TRANSFORMER

Out in the spotlights, Alia was turning slowly from the mike, still riding the rush of applause. For an instant she seemed to look straight at me, as if she knew... An illusion, of course, because I was deep in the wings and she was out there in the dazzle. But with her hair tied back and the spotlights' white glare on her skin, that face...

"Emod?" Dee was whispering again. "Are you sure you're OK?"

The face. The deathmask in the mirror. I hadn't imagined it, it had been there. Yes, it *was* an after-image, and it was impossible, I knew, but still... The face I'd seen was Alia's. It was her.

Point Horror
Unleashed

TRANSFORMER

Philip Gross

SCHOLASTIC

Scholastic Children's Books,
Commonwealth House, 1–19 New Oxford Street,
London WC1A 1NU, UK
a division of Scholastic Ltd
London ~ New York ~ Toronto ~ Sydney ~ Auckland

First published in the UK by Scholastic Ltd, 1996

Copyright © Philip Gross, 1996

ISBN 0 590 13382 9

Typeset by TW Typesetting, Midsomer Norton, Avon
Printed by Cox & Wyman Ltd, Reading, Berks.

10 9 8 7 6 5 4 3 2 1

1

"Alia? Are you down there?"

I peered into the dark beneath the stage. No reply. The spiral stairs were steep, with an iron handrail ending in a knob that might have been a dog's head, snarling.

"Alia?" Out in the hall the crowd was getting restless. There was a whistle or two, and someone tried a slow handclap. It didn't catch on, not this time, but it would. "Alia," I called. "Are you OK?"

"Where's Little Miss Prima Donna, then?" It was Clive. "Oh, I get it. Gone to pieces. Lost her bottle. Folded under pressure. Like I said she would."

"Lay off, Clive," said Ben.

"It was your idea to have her in the first place..." I'll give Clive this: he might not be one of the world's intellectuals, or one of its great guitarists either, but he doesn't give up. Like his bass lines: he just puts his head down and goes thudding from one end of the song to the other. "There was nothing wrong with the old line-up."

"Get a move on, Emod," Ben said. "Go down there and look."

At first it was pitch dark. Then I noticed it – a smear of faint light leaking out beneath the Green Room door. It might have been my eyes, but I thought it flickered slightly, like a bulb about to fuse. "Alia?" I called again. No answer. It was the wrong sort of quiet, like when you suddenly know that someone's looking at you from behind. Overhead the hall was buzzing and shuffling. I could feel it through the floor, like furniture being shifted in a flat upstairs. But there was this silence, the kind you can feel on your skin, behind that door. I felt for the handle and rattled it. Locked. "Hey, Ben," I called back up. "I think there's something wrong."

"Wrong?" Ben hissed, behind me. "You bet there's something wrong. There's about a hundred people out there waiting for a band. Our best crowd yet."

"Well?" Clive called down.

Ben drew a sharp breath. "I said, lay off…"

"Hold it, hold it." Moments like this, that's when they need me. They were getting emotional, and that means trouble. Emod to the rescue. I don't waste time on all this feeling stuff. I reason it out. I took a step back and barged the door.

It gave an inch, and jammed, as if there was something wedged against it.

"Big bands always keep them waiting," Ben said, trying to sound calm. "They do it on purpose. Heightens the expectancy."

"Thanks," snarled Clive. "I'll bear that in mind, next time I'm on with Guns 'n' Roses. This is *us*."

"Help me, you two," I whispered. "Come on, one, two, thr—"

The door swung open. Braced for the big push, the three of us nearly fell at Alia's feet. She was a silhouette, very still, very tall. She always was a big girl, not overweight, just built big, though she used to slouch to make herself seem smaller, same as she used to pull her hair down straight like curtains for her face. Just at that moment, though, she could have been a statue, towering over us, carved from stone.

"Something the matter?" she said in a strange voice, very calm and flat and far away.

Then she was in action, like a film coming out of freeze-frame. She pushed straight past us. "There," I said to Ben. "No prob."

"Hold it," he called after her. "Don't *do* that. Don't just vanish. We were ... we were worried." Clive made a small scoffing noise. Halfway up the spiral stairs she whipped round, drawing her breath in through her teeth. Her knuckles stood out as she gripped the iron bars and for a moment she was a caged thing, crouching. A glint from the stage lights above caught her eyes like a flicker of flame. It was only an instant. When I asked Ben about it after-

3

wards he said he didn't remember. Then she was off up the stairs, with Ben and Clive scrambling after. A moment later there was a cheer and whistling from the crowd. Ben fumbled with the mike and muttered something no one was meant to catch, like real rock bands do, then Geek the drummer crunched into a rhythm, Clive's bass pitched in and the floorboards were an earthquake zone.

I should have been up in the wings, standing by in case a fuse blew. But I didn't move. They didn't need me once the amps were up and running, with their little red lights like bloodshot eyes, once the mikes had been *one-two-one-two*'d. The crowd were there to see Ben's band and this new singer with the odd name, Alia. No one had come to see me. I'm just Emod, the man with the van.

They could have been miles away, the band, the noise. The whole building was shaking like an engine room, cylinders thudding, cogs grinding, pistons punching... But here on the threshold of the Green Room I could feel it, not quite natural, that stillness in the air. Above several hundred watts of heavy metal, I could hear the whisper of a candle flame.

The Green Room. A nowhere sort of place. It smelt like a great-aunt's wardrobe, full of damp and sadness and another bitter smell you couldn't place. The caretaker slung things in here that he'd never get round to mending, just to get them out of sight. Things went in and never came out. Even the name, the Green Room, was a leftover from the days when drama clubs did Shakespeare and pretended to be actors saying things like "Break a leg".

It made me want to whisper, like you do in church. You might not believe a word of it, but go into an empty church and you tiptoe, as if someone just might hear. That was it – a candle... Stupid kid, I thought. Right here under the stage, in a room piled with junk, wood everywhere: a naked flame! Some people just don't *think*.

The floor was a mass of tangling dark shapes, legs of chairs and shadows, criss-crossed like the girders of an iron railway bridge. The back half of a panto-mime horse lay against the concertina folds of an old stage set, resting on the outline of a Scottish castle. A bolt of black lightning cut through the canvas, a real zigzag rip. The horse's head was on a tin trunk with its mouth full of flat wooden teeth wide open, laughing horribly as its wire bones showed through its skin. The place was like some creature's nest, where it dragged back things it had scavenged and left them littered round, half chewed. Bits of *Macbeth* or *Aladdin*, bits of other people's dreams. I tripped on a roll of mouldy carpet, propped up like a body or a drunk behind the door.

Not one candle flame: two... It was a little nightlight in its tin cup, and its own reflection. Behind, the only clue that this had been a dressing-room, was a big arched mirror on the wall. There would have been bulbs all round it like the Big Wheel at the fair, and I imagined little schoolgirl stars of years ago, powdering their faces in the limelight. The bulbs were long gone, and the girls would be withered old grannies, or dead, but Alia had cleared a space in front of the mirror. She had turned the dressing table into a shrine. There was a worm-cast of ash beside the candle – incense – and a faint sharp smell like scorched feathers. That was all, but it felt private, secret: I wasn't meant to be there. And I couldn't look away.

Ker-thud, went the drum. It was a new song, a slow one, a love song. No one thought the words were much cop, except Dee, of course, because Ben had written it for her. Now Alia's voice launched into it, climbing head and shoulders above the backing. A weird girl. People had laughed the first time she had turned up at Ben's garage for a practice. Dee's awkward classmate, twitchy, giggling with shyness, hair tied back in bunches like, well, like a schoolkid. Which she was. People had laughed. But hey, it was true, she could sing.

Someone was watching me, out of the mirror. The dim shape of a man. As I started it started; of course it was me. I leaned closer and a clownish face came at me, lit from beneath in the orangeish glow. It was grotesque, all bottom lip and the tip of the nose, with long shadows smeared upwards like make-up all over its distorted forehead dome. It was a caricature, like a latex puppet of me would be if I'd been famous enough to be worth making fun of on TV. Fat chance of that. This place... It took a thought like that and made it real – too real. I made a face at the ugly mug; it made one back. That's when I knew something was watching us, me and my reflection, from the shadows behind.

"Hey!" I spun round. There was no one, nothing. A trick of the light, an after-image… I turned back to the mirror and I froze. Something hung in the darkness behind me, just a blur at first, then clearer: a face, pale as wax and as still as a deathmask. It was coming slowly into focus like a photo in a tray of fluid in the darkroom of my brain. Developing, changing…

Overhead, the band had hushed and there was Alia's voice climbing, reaching for that high note Ben could never quite make. The mask face was changing, it was coming into focus and the matt white skin was… "No!" I wrenched my gaze away, just as Alia hit that top note, not just hit but smashed it open like a firework exploding while the whole crowd cricks its neck and *oohs* and *aahs*.

"No!" Just in time. As the whole band weighed in with a last huge chord and drum-crash, the rusty old screws must have weakened at last and the big mirror fell towards me. I didn't even hear the smash, but the shock threw me backwards. In the moment's silence before the crowd erupted I lurched for the door. A chair got its legs round mine and I went full length, cursing, blundering like a bull walrus through the junk. Overhead there was a Malibu-sized breaker of applause.

On the stairs, I blinked and screwed my eyes tight but the image from the mirror would not fade. It was a young face, pale, without expression, though the eyes were wide. I could not help it: the sequence replayed, and I watched the eyes getting wider, deeper, till they were two pools of shadow, and the cheeks were shrinking in, with a starved look, thinner and gaunter till the skin was stretched between the cheekbones and the jaw. Stretched till it began to fray. "No!" I gasped again … because the deathmask was alive. It was staring, staring past me in the mirror as if it couldn't take its eyes off itself, and it went on staring as the sunk skin of the cheeks pulled taut, then gave way, ripped and opened, pale lips peeling back in tatters from the teeth that kept their film-star grin.

"Emod?" It was Dee, peering down at me. "Are you OK?" I shook my head. Sweet Dee. Most blokes would give their eye teeth for a moment like this, with Dee's arm round their shoulder, whispering, "Are you OK?" I hardly felt it. "You're bleeding," she said and I touched my cheek, where a little splinter-cut was beginning to sting. I dabbed it with a tissue, but I wasn't thinking about it. I could see through the crack in the curtains, on to the stage.

Out in the spotlights, Alia was turning slowly from the mike, still riding the rush of applause. In rehearsals, she would look at the floor, a shy fifteen-year-old, let the curtains of hair hide her face and mutter, "Was that all right?" Not now. She was still as a lighthouse while the waves broke round her. She was in control. For an instant she seemed to look straight at me, as if she knew... An illusion, of course, because I was deep in the wings and she was out there in the dazzle. But with her hair tied back and the spotlights' white glare on her skin, that face...

"Emod?" Dee was whispering again. "Are you sure you're OK?"

The face. The deathmask in the mirror. I hadn't imagined it, it had been there. Yes, it *was* an after-image, and it was impossible, I knew, but still... The face I'd seen was Alia's. It was her.

2

"Ben, I'm worried about Alia," I said. "Ben? Are you listening?"

Ben detached himself from the huddle round the band. True, most of them were college kids, friends-of-friends or classmates, but they were truly surprised, you could hear it. "Hey, you were *good*!" they'd say, followed by, "And as for that, what's her name… Wow." It was almost as if we had fans.

"I'm worried about Alia," I said again.

"What do you mean?" Ben was getting impatient. "She was great. Even Clive thought so, didn't you, Clive?"

"Yeah, not bad. Not bad at all. If you like that sort of thing…"

"See? What's the problem, Emod?"

That was the question. "It's hard to explain…"

Ben sighed. "Look, we've got a serious adulation

situation here to deal with. So if it's all the same to you…" He grinned and slapped me on the shoulder. Ben and me, we're old mates. "Look, just don't worry. Leave the music to me, and you stick to the wiring, OK?"

We never planned to be a rock band, it just happened. There we were one rainy Sunday afternoon; his stereo had thrown a wobbly and he'd called me in to fix it. He was staring out of the bedroom window. Suddenly he banged his fist on the double glazing so hard that the whole wall shuddered. Most houses in Borsley are made of cardboard. It's that sort of town.

"Something has got to change!"

"Uh?" I said. The tape head needed cleaning, that was all.

"You aren't listening, are you?" he said. "I mean, look at it out there. And look at all this…" He waved an arm around the room. "Don't you ever just want to torch it? Chuck it all in. Leave your clothes on a beach. Run off to … somewhere something really *happens*?"

"No," I said.

He sat down on the bed, hard. "No imagination, that's your problem." Problem? Didn't look that way to me. There was Ben – popular, good looks, good marks, nice place, pretty nice parents considering, and he had this thing about wanting to torch it all and run away. Now, *that's* what I call a problem.

"I don't reckon anybody changes," I said. "I mean,

look at me." He did, and slowly this grin spread round his face. I've never minded being Emod – that's *dome* backwards if you hadn't worked it out already, on account of my head. My English teacher said once that it made me look intellectual. Didn't do much for my Shakespeare, though. It's just the way I am.

"The feeling's quite normal," I said when he'd finished smirking. "Adolescence. There are books about it."

Ben was pacing again. "I'm not staying on at school," he said. "I'm going to sixth-form college."

"Will your mum and dad mind?"

"No, but I'm going to do it anyway. And I'm going to shave my hair up the sides, and have a pigtail. They won't like that."

"You could be in a rock band," I said. "You got Grade Six in guitar."

"That was classical."

"So? I'll fix the amplifiers." And that's what happened. Ben did the hair and went to college (to do three or four A-levels, naturally) and he met Clive, on some day-release course from his garage job, and Clive had a bass, and knew this drummer, Geek, and there they were. I wouldn't say they were stars, but it transformed those rainy Sundays. Sooner or later someone noticed that *Transformer* wasn't a bad name for a band.

That was before Alia. Another world.

It was another of Ben's itchy spells that made it happen. He stood us all a squirt of coffee from the canteen vend-o-mat, so you could tell he had something serious to say. "The band... It isn't going anywhere."

"Dead right. We need an extra thousand watts." That's Clive. He'd move the world, he would, if he had a big enough amp and somewhere to plug it in.

"No, it's the vocals," said Ben.

"You've got a lovely voice," said Dee. Dee is nice. Dee is pretty and quiet and she's got these big brown eyes that watch you as if she really wants to hear what you're saying. Even me. The strange thing is that girls think Dee is nice too, so she really must be.

"I'll do my Metallica imitation," Clive said, not for the first time.

"What I reckon..." Ben ignored them both. "Is we need contrast. Female vocals."

"Oh, Ben..." said Dee. She's got this sweet little voice, has Dee. Sounds quite good in the back of the van, but face her with a microphone... By that Sunday evening everyone agreed. Much as they loved her, Dee was simply, utterly not it.

"I know," she said when they told her. You see, Dee *is* nice. "There's this girl in my class."

"No," Clive said. "Not another choirgirl."

"Wait," said Dee. "She's different..." Alia. Short for Natalia, because her dad was a lecturer in Slavonic Studies somewhere. Only child. That sort of family. But it was true, she was different. And hey, she could sing.

"Where is Alia, anyway?" I said. Ben shrugged. Clive was deep in the fan club scrum. Dee glanced round. "Oh," she said, "she just popped outside for a breath of air."

"Did you think she looked OK?" I said.

"OK?" said Dee. "*OK?* She was great!" I slipped out of the group, not that anyone noticed, and a minute later I was outside in the cool night air. People were straggling off in pairs and small groups. I couldn't see Alia. I thought I'd find her on the steps or in the car park, just taking a breather, but no. It was dark, the college grounds were practically deserted, and for the first time I noticed how this place, this ordinary place I come to most days, was strange.

Apart from the old hall most of the college was see-through – boxes of concrete and plate glass that looked modern in the Sixties, piled like ice-cubes three storeys high. You could look right through the science block. As I looked, the wing-flash, red-white, of a plane on the run-in to Luton passed across it, and I couldn't tell whether it was a reflection in the glass or in the sky beyond. The noise arrived a moment later, rising through the constant mutter of the motorway spur, like the faint growl in a sleeping dog's throat. For a moment I thought: that's Borsley all over. It's a trick they do with mirrors. Nothing's really here at all.

Round the side of the hall was tarmac that had

been a playground when this was a school. Two basketball posts stood glinting weirdly white, though there wasn't a moon, just the rusty glow of streetlights. Suddenly a side door banged open as somebody leaned on the Fire Exit bar. With a shriek of laughter, four or five girls emptied from the bright yellow light into the darkness, and the sweat-hot air of the dancefloor billowed out round them like smoke from a furnace. The door slammed shut, they reeled off chattering, and the yard was cool and still again.

It was round another corner, between the back of the hall and the canteen kitchens, that I saw them. Alia and...? I ducked out of sight between industrial-size bins with hatches like tanks and steel wheels. Carefully, I peered out. The smell of a whole week's dinners going rotten hung around me in the air.

Her dad, come to fetch her? I'd seen him, a meek man with stooped shoulders. No, it wasn't him. Alia's tall, as I said, and standing proud this eve-ning, but the shape beside her was a whole head taller. Boyfriend? There was no such animal, we had Dee's word for that. "I keep on trying to fix her up," Dee said. "But the moment she starts talking all the boys get scared and run away." I peered between the bins. I couldn't see clearly, but the figure with her wasn't a boy; it was a man.

I couldn't go back. I was lucky they hadn't seen me straight away as I came round the corner. So I slipped along in the shadow of the line of bins. Further down was a wire cage, a crate on wheels, half full of boxes, cartons, paper for recycling, and I came up cautiously to look between the bars. In the middle of the yard was a narrow splash of light from the hall's back window, but it didn't light the two of them. If anything, it made the darkness where they stood more deeply dark.

They were shadows, a metre apart. They didn't speak. Somehow they didn't look like friends. They might just have been lovers in a white-hot tiff, but that wasn't quite it either. They were facing each other, very upright, almost formal, like partners in an ancient dance or ritual. He was looking down at her, so huge and still, and his gaze so steady, that I expected her to flinch or look away, but no... She was meeting his stare; there was a force field in the air between them, like between poles of a magnet, so strong you could almost see it.

Then without warning he bowed his head slightly, and she bowed hers, like a solemn agreement, and his right arm came out and rested on her shoulder very slowly, as if he might stroke her hair or snap her neck with a single twist, whichever the ritual demanded. Then he laughed. "So you see," he said in a low voice with rough edge. "You can fly." There was a low crumbling sound as the next jet on the Luton flight path winked across the night sky. They both looked up and though his face was still in darkness I saw the flash of his teeth, large and uneven, as he smiled. Then she turned without a word and walked towards me. Her face flashed in the light of the window, and her eyes were serious and bright. Then she was gone, round the corner, going back towards the hall, as if nothing had happened. As for me, I didn't budge an inch.

For a minute or two the man just stood there, half in shadow, sharing that silent grin of his with no one in particular. They weren't going to be seen together, that was for sure. At last he turned on his heel, moving his bulk surprisingly fast, and with a slow lope came my way. He passed through the light from the window, and just for a moment there was his face above me, an arm's reach away, through the bars of my rubbish-bin cage.

It wasn't an ugly face, with its stubble, its long dented profile, its chin like a fist; words like ugly or handsome just didn't apply. That face had power; it was grand and half in ruins, with its cracks and creases deepened by the angle of the light. It was a still face, not a flicker of expression, like a carving in a desert, eaten at by sand and time. But not old. His long hair was dark, dragged back Native American-style, roughly tied with a thong. The leather of his coat was not the stylish kind but rough and heavy, with raw edges showing like an unhealed wound. It was fastened with a clasp, not buttons, at his throat. Then he was out of the light. A moment later came the cough and throttle of a heavy motorbike.

Back in the hall, the huddle of fans was still tight

around the others, and I could see that Alia was in the thick of it. There were notebooks out, and diaries too; someone from the local listings mag was there, and a man from a club, and we had a booking, not a college bop, a real venue. Whatever it was Alia had – and wherever it came from – the world wanted more.

3

"Where does she go?" I said. "I mean, when we don't see her. What does she do with herself?"

"Not much," said Dee. "She reads books. Works. She's a real keener at school."

"Yes, but..." How could I even start on this? "That can't be all."

Ben and Dee were sitting on the kerb of the little fountain that made it sound as if it was raining, even on sunny days, in the new shopping mall. Under the choppy water all the pebbles were exactly the same size. The underwater light bulbs were not quite hidden by the imitation pondweed that was one shade too bright green. The security man walked past, quite close, every now and then, to make sure we knew he had his eye on us. It was nothing personal; he did it to anyone under thirty. Above us, silver escalators hummed and lines of shoppers popped up off them and toddled off like things from a production line.

"She does an evening class, I think. No boy-friend, if that's what you mean," said Dee with a meaningful look.

"Come off it," I said and we all laughed, Ben loudest, though not very comfortably. He fished for a pebble, frowning. As usual, Alia was late.

"Seriously," he said. "I think she's a great find for the band. Not sure if Clive agrees, though." Clive and Geek, they just wanted to be old-time rockers in an old-time rock band. They tuned their brains out when Alia started on about crop circles or reincarnation, but when she got on to animal rights and told Clive he ought to burn his leather jacket, he flipped.

"He'll see, though," said Ben. "The next gig's going to be something special. Alia's got some new ideas." He gave up on the pebble. I could have told him that they came in a unit, all the fountains had them, welded in one piece.

"I'll go and look for her," said Dee. Alia was her friend, after all. "She'll be on the wrong level, knowing her."

"Look at it all!" said Ben, as soon as Dee was out of sight. "All these zombies! The high point of their week! This is the most exciting place in Borsley, can you imagine it?"

"It's just a place," I said.

"Place? It's not a place. It's nowhere, nothing,

noplace, zilch." He kicked the fountain. "Somebody stuck a pin in a map and said: let's have a New Town ... there."

"Ben," I said. "The other night ... Alia... Don't you think it was strange? I mean, she can sing. But she's never been like *that*..."

He laughed. "Are you complaining?"

"It was eerie," I said.

"It was wild."

"I'm worried, that's all. What if she's into ... into something dangerous?" Ben was fed up with this, I could see. But I wanted to say it when Dee was out of earshot. "After the gig," I said, "I followed her outside..."

"Oh-ho," Ben grinned. "Dee was right."

"Leave off. I'm serious. She sneaked off to meet someone, out at the back. This man. They didn't do anything at all, just stood. Then he said something weird. He said: *you can fly*."

Ben stared into the fountain. "You mean, you think she was *on* something? Drugs, is that it? Did you see him give her something?" I shook my head. Dee appeared at the top of the escalator. Suddenly Ben chuckled. "All I can say is: if there's a drug that makes you sing like that, give me some of it. Come on, Emod, she's the best thing the band's ever had. The other night," he said, quickly, with one eye out for Dee approaching. "On stage ... I've never felt anything like it. As if we were all ... all..." He tailed off with a wave of the arms.

"Flying?" I suggested.

Dee flopped herself down on the side of the fountain so it shook. Just then, as if from thin air, Alia appeared. She was her gawky, fifteen-year-old self again, straight from an after-school hockey match, with her face still blotchy round the cheeks from running and her hair in bunches done up with elastic bands. A straight zero score for style and sex-appeal. She cast a sharp look round the mall. "We can't talk here," she said, without even a *Hi*. "Come with me."

When the new mall landed in Borsley town centre, it was like a bomb going off, but slowly. Two blocks were flattened and a crater appeared, four or five storeys deep. There was talk about archaeological evidence, but they never found any, not a trace that anyone had ever lived here before. Ben was right: this was nowhere.

At the back of the mall was an acres-wide Pay & Display. We zigzagged across it now, in and out of the ranks of parked cars, while the warden watched us with her notebook in her hand. On the opposite side was a row of older houses, battered and bricked in and chopped off at the end, as though they'd been condemned but the contractors couldn't be bothered to put them out of their misery. That was where Alia led us. Come to think of it now, she was always leading us into darker and pokier places. But Ben was so fed up with Borsley, he didn't object.

Half the windows of the row were boarded up.

The end wall was painted black all over and propped up with thick beams like a massive wooden crutch. It must have been an inside wall once, because you could see traces of a staircase and a fireplace ten metres up. The tarry black paint dribbled round the corner and someone had daubed ARCANA over the café door.

A smell of coffee and baking hit us as we stepped in. We had to duck, and I stayed in a crouch because it felt so dark and small. Under the smells of food I thought I caught a hint of that bitter incense in the air, and I shuddered. Whatever I'd seen in the Green Room that night, I couldn't explain it. I was trying to give up trying to, but it was hard. Especially when I saw what I saw next.

"What sort of place *is* this?" Dee whispered.

"Vegetarian," said Alia. She seemed perfectly at home.

"Then what's all *that*?" said Dee.

On the wall, a life-size painting of a skeleton looked us in the eye. In and out of its rib cage coiled a golden snake. Its body corkscrewed up the spine, to burst out of the top of the skull with fangs bared and cobra hood flaring, straight towards us. "Oh, that's Kundalini," said Alia casually. "The life force. Indian, you know?" I didn't, but then again it hadn't really been a question. I was bending down to look at several shelves of things that seemed to be for sale. There were twenty different sets of tarot cards, with images of falling towers struck by lightning, hanged men and the skeleton again. There were soot-coloured candles that looked at first like lumps of coal. When I looked closer I saw they were skulls. When they burned down the flames would flicker through the eye-sockets, as if something in there was alive. "Ben?" said Dee quietly, "I don't like this." She put her hand in his.

"Hi, there, what would you like?" It was a voice with no expression. The thin man at the counter had a stringy beard and hair so pale it was almost colourless, as though he had grown inside these boarded-up windows like a mushroom farm. One of the Beansprout People, I thought. "They'll all have coffee," said Alia without asking. "I'll have comfrey tea." She twanged the elastic bands out of her bunches and shook her hair loose. In the twilight of the café she was suddenly relaxed, her voice growing more and more lively as she spoke.

The Beansprout poured our coffees slowly, laid them on the counter slowly, one by one, then stood. As Alia shepherded us to a table I could feel those pale eyes watching, probably not thinking anything but taking it all in, like the way sheep look up when you pass their field. After a moment he started to slice green peppers slowly, sleepwalker-style, with a long wicked knife.

"Well, do you like it?" said Alia.

"Uh…" I mumbled. "It's got atmosphere."

Then all of a sudden she was talking – music stuff, something about a tape she'd heard of

Mongolian chanting, and whale song, and the things you can do with synthesizers these days, and shamanic drumming, and if only we could get away from the old rock line-up we could really...

I was on the sidelines. Ben was in the thick of it. "...Clive and Geek won't like it," I heard him say after a while.

Alia shrugged. "I don't know if we need them."

"Wait a minute..." Dee spoke up, blushing a little, like she does when she's afraid there might be an argument. But she spoke up, all the same. "Clive and Geek are our friends."

Alia gave her a straight look. "If you want to be a bunch of friends who practise in a garage," she said, "that's all right by me. But you don't need me. I want to make music. Real music, like nobody's heard before. Ben, don't you agree?"

"Well," Ben said, "yes, but..."

"Then nothing else matters," said Alia. "It could really happen. It *was* happening the other night. I could feel it. Couldn't you?" And they were deep in conversation, talking fast to each other straight across the table. Ben was leaning forward more and more, as if there was some kind of force field, something her eyes gave out, that was sucking him in. Dee didn't speak again, but after a while she got up and walked over to the tarot packs and candles. She studied them too carefully, too long. By the time I went over, casually, and stood beside her, Ben and Alia were deep in rewriting a song.

"Is she always like this?" I said. "What's she like at school?"

"She's my friend," said Dee, as if that was an answer. "I'm glad someone's listening to her for a change. At school they just take the mick or avoid her. She's always walking in and saying, 'I've been reading about this tribe who...' – oh, boil their ancestors' brains or something – when all the others want to talk about is *Neighbours*." Dee turned from the lumpy skull-candles to me. "You've got to understand. They gave her a really hard time at her old school, that's why her parents moved her. And they're pretty peculiar too. It's just always the same for her: she never fits."

I nodded. I know a bit about that. "It's no better with boys," Dee went on. "I try to take her to parties and things. It never really works, I don't know why." I could have told her. Boys like girls like Dee. Dee makes them feel strong and smart and in control of things. Whereas a girl like Alia...

"I mean," she said. "Take you. You don't fancy her, do you?"

"Me? That's different. I don't fancy anyone, not very much." I glanced at Dee quickly, to see if this was the wrong thing to say. Most things are the wrong things to say to girls, I find. But she was just looking at me, sort of sympathetic. "I ... I just don't seem to have that circuit wired in," I said. "That's all."

"That must make life a lot easier," said Dee, with

feeling. "And she *is* my friend," she added quickly, looking back towards Alia and Ben.

"OK," said Ben as we got back to the table. "I'll try and talk Clive round. We'll give it a go."

"Alia?" I said carefully. "That gig the other night. What *did* it feel like, up there?"

She looked at me hard, as if she'd just noticed me for the first time. "What's it *like*?" she said. She held her hand out with her elbow on the table, fingers clenched in a fist. Very slowly, she unclenched it, as if there was something in there she wanted to show me, something very secret, or alive.

"Power," she said. I was still looking at her outstretched hand, with the marks, first white then red, that her nails had left in the palm. For a second I had a flash of something, a trick of the light, because her curling fingers with the sharp nails were a claw, a bird's claw, fastening on nothing, just flexing for now as it looked for its prey.

"Power," she said again. "You can do anything." Suddenly I couldn't breathe, it was stuffy and close in there, that tiny room that felt like underground. It felt crowded to bursting point, suffocating, although there was no one in there except us, and the Beansprout gazing at us from the counter, and the Kundalini skeleton from the wall.

"Anything!" said Alia. "You can fly."

4

It was rattling the bars of its cage. What it was I couldn't see because there was just the single candle burning in the middle of the floor; the cage hung in an alcove like an archway leading back and down. What kind of bird could need a cage like that? It was big as a wardrobe, with bars thick as railings, but it shuddered and I didn't want to but I had to look. As I reached towards the cage my shadow reached out with me, touched it first, and with a clash something hurled itself against the bars and lashed out, screeching. No! I screamed as a hooked claw ripped my shadow from me, snatching it into the cage. A grey feather fluttered slowly past me and I stared into the darkness where there still was nothing I could see.

There were other dreams like that. Some nights, to

keep them off, I'd lie awake but the moment I shut my eyes there'd be that face, very nearly a skull but still alive. Alive and smiling. I'd jerk upright in bed and put the light on; I'd plug myself into talk radio for half the night, anything to keep those thoughts at bay.

I couldn't tell Ben. It would sound crazy. Anyway, he was getting all defensive when I mentioned Alia these days – almost as edgy as she used to be. Sometimes he'd look vacant for a moment, then, "Think," he'd say. "If I could play guitar like she can sing..." There was nothing else for it: I had to go back and look.

I eased the handle of the Green Room door, as if someone might hear. Maybe the caretaker had been down and found the broken mirror? Maybe he'd find me now and say: *so it was you*! I'd crept through the hall as the badminton club were setting up their nets and when no one was looking I slipped backstage, feeling for the cold iron handrail as I felt my way downstairs. I took a deep breath, put out my hand and tried the door.

There had to be a simple answer. Like it must have been Clive's mega-wattage up on stage; it loosened the mirror fixtures in the wall. As for the face... Well, couldn't it have been a kind of *déjà vu*? I mean, that's when you see something and you think you've seen it before, but you haven't. That night I thought I saw something for the first time, when I hadn't ... *yet*, until I saw her face on stage.

That's impossible. Forget it, Emod. Just open the door.

It didn't creak. It just came open and there was the same old clutter, not strange at all now, simply cluttered, simply old. It wasn't even dark; glimmers of daylight came in through the cracks in the walls and the stage. It didn't have that shrine-room feeling any more. Whatever that was, it had been to do with Alia, not the place.

And the mirror was still on the wall.

Oh God, I thought, it's me. I really am crazy. Or I dreamed it. That felt better. Nothing happened at all. Another case of *déjà*-not-quite-*vu*.

I looked in the mirror. That took a bit of an effort, but there was just my reflection, nothing stranger than that. In front of the mirror there was that same little worm-cast of joss-stick ash, the tin cup of the nightlight, burned out, and a greyish feather. For a moment I couldn't catch my breath, as though that same burnt smell was in the air. My dream, I thought. The feather. And in the same flicker of pictures through my skull I saw Alia's hand, in the café, making a point about something, fingers curling and clenching. "Power," she'd said. For the first time, I noticed quite how thin her fingers were, how bony. Like a bird's, a hawk's, a raptor's claw.

I slammed the lid of my mind shut firmly. Don't think about it, OK. Dreams and weird stuff. Just don't think, that's all.

* · * · *

I was late to the garage, out of breath from running. "Hi," called Ben. "You getting into training?" But I could see he was nervous. This was the last time we would get together before the club gig. The new things still sounded scrappy and ragged, but everyone agreed: this would be the rehearsal that made the difference. In a way, it was.

Ben's parents lived in the Rat Run, one of those car-free developments of little houses Lego-bricked together with high walls so no one ever sees anyone else. All the lanes looked like back alleys, and you got the feeling that if you got mugged there one night no one would open their doors. After all, it was a cut above most of Borsley. People like Ben's family had paid good money for a bit of privacy.

The good thing about the place was that there were lock-up garages, out on the edge of the lanes, well out of earshot of the neighbours. Ben had a deal with his parents; he washed the car on a Sunday morning and the rest of the day we used the garage for the band.

There was only one power point out there but I got us a bunch of adaptors and soon we were plugged in and humming. "What's this club like, anyway?" I asked.

"Nothing special," Ben said. "The kind of place schoolkids go with forged ID. Still, it's a gig." Just then Dee burst in with something in her hand. "You've made it," she said. It was this week's issue of the local listings paper, and we had a whole half-page on us. OK, ninety-five per cent of it was about Alia, but still…

"Never mind," said Clive. "Just as long as it mentions the gig. Nobody *reads* these things anyway." He turned up his amp and went into a bass line like a ton of bricks.

Alia was a real hard worker, you had to agree. Sometimes we'd go over the same song ten times and still she'd want to try it one more time. "Oh, come off it," Ben snapped once, "it's good enough."

She rounded on him. "*Good enough*'s not good enough for me. There's no point in doing it if it isn't perfect."

Other times she'd be the same old Alia we'd met on the very first evening. Dee's shy friend. "She isn't exactly *pretty*," Dee had warned us in advance. "But she's sort of interesting." Alia dressed, pick'n'mix, from things she picked up second-hand, good bargains. Sometimes it looked stylish. Other times she looked like an explosion in an Oxfam shop.

This rehearsal, though… They really went for it, hour after hour. It was a hot day, thundery, with that sort of electric feeling in the air, and everyone was sweating. The garage felt smaller than it had ever done before, and people kept tripping over leads. "Oy," said Geek for the twentieth time, "don't crowd me, right?" and Ben snarled back at him, and I had to do my "Hey guys, let's all cool it" act. By the time they all noticed they were tired it was dark outside.

There was just the one song left to do, the slow one, the one I'd noticed Alia really *fly* on, that night at the college. It seemed to be going OK, when suddenly she stopped. "Hold it," she said. "Ben, I need a word with you."

They were in the corner, backs turned to us, for five minutes, more. Geek had popped his last beer can and Clive was giving warning plunks on his bottom string. I went over.

"I know, I know…" Ben was saying. "But nobody *hears* the words anyway."

"*I* hear them," Alia said. "That matters. Anyway, I'm only changing a few words." Ben was staring at a scrap of crumpled paper, full of Alia's jagged writing. "What was wrong with the old version?" he said.

"*I'm so in love, I love you so,*
I'm never going to let you go…
You mean that bit?" said Alia, withering him.

"Well…" Ben squirmed. "Oh, come on, it was only meant to be a love song."

She gave an I-give-up sort of shrug. "Another pretty love song! Like all the rest. *Oooh, baby.* Don't you want to be different?"

"Well, yes, but…" He caught sight of me standing there. "OK," he said. "We'll try it your way. Just to see."

Alia let the creeping footsteps of the bass and drums build up, very slowly, then she hit her first note, low and soft as the purr of a tiger in its cage. It seemed to be a love song. Ben's chords came in, nervously, I thought, till Alia's left hand gestured *harder, sharper*. Her face was lifted but her eyes were closed. That icy edge was in her voice. That first gig, it had been there for a moment in the last verse. Now it was there from the start. It *seemed* to be a love song…

I love you and you'll never know…

One hand closed round the mike as if to stroke it, then her fingers tightened suddenly, clenched round its throat. That man, at the back of the hall, with his hand on her shoulder, that night…

I'll cover you like falling snow…

This was soft, half sexy, half a lullaby. She let her head loll a little and her eyes closed. Her lips went tight and narrow, in what might have been a smile except it was too hard, too still and showed too many teeth.

*I'll freeze your heart and I'll never let go
and we'll lie in the ground tonight.*

Dee was scrambling to her feet and pushing past me. "Need some air," she muttered, making for the small door at the back. She jogged the shelf and something fell, but the bass and drums were gathering for the climax, and only the smell of white spirit told me anything had happened. As they hit the last verse, I was slipping out behind her. "What's wrong, Dee?"

The air was cold after the fug of the garage, and I could see Dee's breath like steam. "It's horrible,

horrible.". She didn't look at me. "That's my song," she said. "Alia's got no right…" In films there are moments like this. The guy says the right thing, or rests his hand on her shoulder, or… Me, I just stood.

"And Ben!" she said. "That's what gets me. *Ben*…"

"Dee," I said. "You can't … you can't think that…"

"Go on, say it!"

I swallowed. "You can't think that Ben … I mean that Ben really *likes* her."

"That he fancies her, you mean. No, of course not!" Her voice came out shrill. "Nobody fancies Alia. I mean, if it wasn't for me… Of course he doesn't fancy her. I mean, it's ridiculous." There was a pause. "It *is* ridiculous, Emod, isn't it?"

"No. I mean, yes, it is. Ridiculous."

"Talk to him," Dee said. "You're his friend." She was looking straight at me with those big eyes all the boys fall backwards over.

"I'll try," I said. "Now let's get back inside."

They were doing it one more time, and just reaching the last verse again. All the lads were bent over their instruments, so Alia rose above them all. I thought of the Statue of Liberty, with tugs and liners going to and fro beneath her feet, and her face is a mask, and hollow, with tiny people peering out through the slots in her crown.

Who was Alia? What was she doing to us all? And what had she done to herself? It wasn't just that she started standing up and looking people in the eye. It wasn't that she'd shed her clutter of jumble sale clothes and started wearing plain things, very black and trim. She had actually changed. The shape of her face was leaner, and her cheeks had lost that little-girl plumpness and were pale in a way that made her eyes darker, larger and deeper so the force of them hit you when she looked at you. Magnificent, but...

She was more like the face in the mirror.

"Hey!" There was a sudden squall of voices and the music trailed off in mid-verse. "You touched my amp!" said Clive.

"I told you: you've got to be quiet there," said Alia.

"What are you talking about? That's the build-up, really powerful."

"*Powerful?* You call that powerful? That's just noise. They've got to hear the voice."

"Just you, eh? Ben, Geek and me, we can go home?"

She just looked at him, dead cold. That's when Clive flicked his volume up to full. The air buzzed and the speakers quivered, ready to scream with feedback. "Go back to school, kid. People want to hear a *beat*." Clive glanced at Geek and together they crashed into a heavy metal thing. Whatever Alia started saying, and whatever Ben was shouting at them both, and Dee's small sobs and my "Hey guys, cool it..." were swamped in a damburst of noise. Alia lunged for Clive's amp, but he stepped into the way to block her. I don't think he meant it but he swung round with his bass and the machine-heads caught her on the face so she staggered sideways, clutching her cheek. The mike stand went over with a thunder-crack and Alia was swaying for a moment, bringing her hand away from her face, and staring at it, dumbstruck. It was only a scratch, but there was blood.

She didn't make a move towards Clive, not this time. She drew herself up to full height. She raised her arm, as if to point, not with a finger but a fist, and not quite a fist either, but that gesture from the café, fingers curled into a claw. Clive's fingers faltered on the fretboard, though Geek's drums banged on. A whine of feedback started. In that moment Alia took a breath and screamed.

I've heard girls scream before, I mean not just play at screaming but really do it, in a playground fight. This was different. This was something else. It wasn't a girl's scream at all but the scream of a bird, a hawk, a wild thing dropping on its prey, and it cut right through the drums and the howl of the feedback. Clive staggered back. There was a blue flash and a sizzling *phwap*!

We were struggling in darkness, f-words every-where, as all of us blundered towards where we thought the door might be. Geek's high-hat went over, glancing off my kneecap like a close shave with a guillotine. There was a papery thump as some-one's foot went through a speaker. Ben was trying to shout, "Calm down, everybody!" but his voice was panicky, then he tripped over somebody else and he swore too.

"Hold it," he said. "I've got a light." As he clicked his lighter on the small flame leaped to the floor and went jiggling about in a broad sheet, ghostly blue. The white spirit. Dee shrieked once and started whimpering. Then there was a grating rattle and the garage door hinged up and over, letting in the light.

Ben's father was squinting in at us. "What the hell have you done?" he yelled. "You've blown every fuse in the house."

In the long pause that followed he surveyed the wreckage. There was the gear and the drum kit all over the floor, broken glass, the smell of burning, and us crawling through it all on hands and knees. All but Alia, that is. She hadn't moved. The orange streetlight caught her as she looked around, looked down at us all. It could have been that moment on the stage again, with all the spotlights on her, and the streets outside were filled with silent applause.

Very slowly, she smiled. I closed my eyes. I knew that smile. I'd seen it. In the Green Room. It would go on, getting wider, tighter till the cheeks ripped and the skull showed through the skin. Then I blinked, and it was just Alia, looking puzzled now, the awkward kid who's spoiled the party though she doesn't quite see how.

Don't get me wrong: I'm not one of your mystic-artistic types, no way. I believe in explanations. But the only explanation that made sense, at that moment, was that *she had made it happen*. Somehow.

That was when I started to be worried about Alia for real.

5

"What do you mean: *talk about last night?*" Ben snapped. All I'd said was maybe we should talk about … what happened.

"Nothing *happened*," he said. "We just blew a fuse, that's all. Dad says you need your head examined, jamming all those adaptors in one socket." He was striding on so fast I had to keep putting in a little skip and scurry just to keep up. "No damage to the amps, anyway," I ventured. "Was Geek OK about the drum?"

"Not very," said Ben. "I think he wants out."

"Why? The band's just starting to take off." Ben did not reply. "Oh," I said, "it's Alia, isn't it?"

He stopped dead. Instead of turning to face me Ben picked up a stone and threw it, hard and vicious, at the huddle of seagulls out in the mud in the middle of the playing field. They went up like smoke from a small bomb, then planed off down-wind to the landfill site. Little dumptrucks trundle to and fro all day, unloading Borsley's rubbish with a rattle that reaches you a second later, like a time warp. Ben looked up into thin air. "Listen to that," he said.

There was a buzzing all around us; we were underneath the power line. It's so much part of the Borsley skyline you don't see it any more. In the distance the pylons looked almost graceful, like old-fashioned girls curtseying with loops of wire like ribbons and bows. They came in a straight line from one horizon to the other, stepping over Borsley on the way without noticing it, on their way to London from the nuclear reactor on the coast.

"Power," he said. Each pylon wore a row of brown ceramic bangles – insulators. From one just above us came a crackling, splashing sound.

The way he said it, I remembered Alia in the café. *Power*... That's what she said too. "Ben," I said. "We've got to talk about Alia."

He whipped round. "Look, stop going on about her, OK? What's everybody got against her? Just because she's the only person in this town who *thinks*..."

I bit my lip. "Dee isn't very happy," I said.

Ben's jaw locked. "What about Dee?" he said between his teeth.

"She ... she *is* your girlfriend, after all."

Ben's lip curled. "You!" he said. "You ... telling

me what to do with women. You, with your vast experience!"

That hurt. Still, I muttered, "Sometimes Dee talks to me."

"Oh yeah? Only because you're safe," he sneered. "She reckons you're probably gay." He swung on his heel and marched off. "Just leave off about Alia," he snarled back over his shoulder and left me staring out over Borsley. All the little square pieces, and the piled blocks of the mall. It looked like a construction set some giant kid had played with once, and might come back to tidy up one day.

"Sorry," said Ben. "I didn't mean it." It was just after supper when he called round. "Truth is, the others have been getting at me too." He looked at the doorstep. "I thought … I thought maybe I'd better have a word with her."

"Dee?"

"No, stupid. Alia. I'm going round there now."

"Wait a mo," I said. "I'm coming with you." For a moment his jaw clenched again, then he smiled: "Fair enough. You think the kid's kind of spooky, don't you? Luring poor boys to their doom. Let's cure you of this thing you've got about her. You just come along and see."

It was out on the west end of town, where the houses had names not numbers, but I saw at a glance that it wouldn't exactly be posh. There were thickets of weeds in the garden that looked as if someone had gone at them with a machete and given up halfway. The front curtains weren't drawn and through the window I could hardly see the room for boxes full of files and papers, avalanching piles of books, a couple of music stands on their sides like giant stick insects, and an empty cello case. We knocked.

"Excuse me," said Ben as the door swung open. He was on his best behaviour. "I'm Ben and…"

"Ben!" The woman clapped her hands like a small girl at a party. "I've heard so much about you." Her hair was a frizz that might have been permed once. Now it looked like springs exploding from a broken clock. "Do step inside. Pardon the mess. In a bit of a fluster, sorry. I'm her mum, by the way." There was a smell of scorching stir-fry from the kitchen.

"Are we interrupting supper?" Ben said. "We just wondered if Alia was in."

"Oh…" She frowned a moment. "We thought she was with you. Well, never mind. She never tells me where she's going. John?" she shouted at the kitchen door. "Where's Natalia, do you know?"

The door opened a crack, with a cloud of steam, and a tall thin man bobbed out. He had a fuzz of grey hair and gold-rimmed glasses. "No, dear, I thought you did. Must be at her meditation."

"Meditation?" I said.

"You know," she said. "The people from the café…"

"The café…" I guessed. "The Arcana?"

"That's the place." Alia's mother leaned forward and lowered her voice. "I do think it's good for her, a bit of relaxation. She works too hard, it worries us sometimes. She's just got to be top at everything. That's why it's nice she's in your pop group, have a bit of fun. Must be good for her, don't you think?"

Did I think? No, I was trying not to. Trying not to see that freeze-frame moment at the first gig, Alia's face white in the spotlight like some priestess ready for the sacrifice. Or the sizzle of lightning in the garage just as everything blew. *Nice she's in your pop group, have a bit of fun...* Were they talking about Alia? There was something terrible about that kid, something scary and, yes, sort of wonderful. And the strangest thing was that no one seemed to see the power in her but me.

Ben cut in. "So that's where she'll be, then, at the café?"

"I should think so. Though it's usually Thursdays, meditation. Still, she's a law unto herself, our Natalia..."

We were backing out of the door. "Well, so nice to meet you," Alia's mother burbled, "Ben. And ... sorry, I didn't catch your name?"

"Emod."

"Emod," she said vaguely. "That's nice."

Then we were out on the pavement. "See," said Ben. "Nothing spooky... Emod, what are you thinking?"

I shook my head. I was thinking: *Her mum and*

dad don't know her any more than we do. No one...
(The thought of the man in the car park loomed at me, that ruined Red-Indian face; I pushed it aside.) *No, no one knows that girl at all.*

"Hi, there," said the Beansprout. "What can I do you?" The café looked more like a mushroom farm than ever in the evening light. Hollow panpipe music huffed and quivered in the background. There were four or five other Beansprouts at the tables chatting, but no Alia. It didn't look like a meditation group to me.

"Just looking for a friend." Ben scanned the shadows.

"Sure," said the Beansprout mildly. "What's she look like?"

I could see Ben hesitate. Asked point blank like that, it wasn't easy to say what Alia looked like. Which Alia, anyway? The schoolgirl in her bunches? Or that marble mask on stage? Or...

"Well," said Ben. "She's sort of tall ... and she *talks*..." As he said it, Ben's right hand opened in a gesture. Opened and closed: the same gesture Alia made when she said the word "power".

"Oh, you mean Alia," said the Beansprout. "Sorry, not been in tonight." I looked at his eyes. Had there been a worried flicker there?

"She said something about a meditation class," said Ben.

Yes, certainly a flicker. The Beansprout shrugged

his nonexistent shoulders. "Don't know. There are dozens." He pointed at the small ad board beside the counter. Every other card said something *Meditation* or *The Way of* something. One said simply *Transform Your Life*.

"Any luck?" The Beansprout came over. He had sold a slice of carrot cake, and seemed exhausted by the effort. But he was keeping an eye on us, I was sure. Ben shook his head.

"Bad luck," said the Beansprout. "Hope you find her," easing us towards the door. Then I took a shot in the dark.

"She's with ... you know, the big guy." I pulled both hands back through my hair and mimed the way he wore it in a thong. The man in raw leather, in the shadows of the hall that night.

The Beansprout stopped dead. Looked at me closely. Very closely. Waiting. I'd started now, so I had to go on.

I lowered my voice. "She's been *learning to fly*."

"You know ... Hugo?" said the Beansprout, in a low voice, as if even the name was too heavy to lift.

"Sure," I said quickly, before Ben could shake his head again. "We've met."

The Beansprout's eyes flickered in Ben's direction. "Him too?"

Ben looked confused. This bit was up to me. "He's interested," I said. The Beansprout frowned, not quite convinced.

"Dunno," he said. "Better check it out first. Ring

him. You got his number?"

"I did," I lied. "I lost it." The Beansprout's pale eyes fixed me for a moment, then he jerked his head towards the notice-board.

"The one that says *Transform Your Life…*"

"You just listen," said Ben. "I'll do the talking." He had rifled my pockets for 10p pieces and there was a pile of them balanced ready for a long call. Or it could be very short.

"Don't mention Alia," I whispered. I didn't know why, though it might have been something to do with the way they looked at each other in the shadows that night, her and this Hugo. Something unspoken. And the way the Beansprout had looked at us just now. Whoever he was, I guessed, one hint that we were interfering and that phone would go down with a clunk, and we'd have lost him. More important, we'd have lost the secret half of Alia too.

Ben dialled. Through the back of the handset I could hear the ringing tone. I gazed across the car park. It was dark, or as dark as it gets, and empty except for one car with a dumped look. One or two people came out of the Arcana café, and there was a glimmer from the door, but the windows were sealed like the blackout in the war. The middle of Borsley: four hours ago it was seething with shoppers, office people, kids bunking off school… Now it was no-man's-land. Things crept out of alleys to scavenge, though you never saw them; that car had lost its rubber trim and wipers already. A couple of days and the tyres would be gone. By the time the council came to tow it away there'd be only a burnt shell left. The phone rang on.

"No answer," Ben said.

"Give him a chance." I didn't relish the next bit either, but we were hooked. If he didn't answer this time, we would have to ring again. It might as well be now.

Click. The tone stopped. No one spoke. Ben cleared his throat. "Hello?" Ben said. "Hello? It's about the advert. In the café."

"Ah, yes..." It was him, no doubt about it. The face might have been battered, but that voice was slow and precise. It was a doctor's bedside manner when he's just about to break the bad news.

"Is, is it some kind of class?" Ben said. "I'm interested in ... meditation, things like that..."

"Something like that," said the voice, slowly. "But ... are you serious?"

Ben swallowed. "Yes," he said.

"Easy to say." The voice waited. Ben took a deep breath. "It's Borsley," he said, all in a rush. "It's so empty. There's got to be more to life than this." That wasn't in the script. He meant it.

"Yes..." Just a hint of a smile in the voice, maybe. We were in. "I must warn you, we don't tolerate dabblers. I expect my students to work hard. To be disciplined. To take certain risks." His voice was very soft now, so I had to lean close. "There are always risks," he purred, "when you're dealing with power."

Ben was sounding as calm as he could. "Power?" he said.

There was the slightest chuckle at the other end. "The power, for example, to see things clearly. Just as I can see your young friend standing next to you." I jumped back, catching my head on the side of the booth. Ouch. Ben was holding the phone out to me. "He wants to talk to you," he whispered.

"Rub it better," the voice said, teasing coldly. "Do I take it your friend speaks for the two of you?"

"Yes."

"We shall see," he said. *Bip-bip-bip* … the phone went. Ben and I grabbed for the 10ps. They went clattering on the floor.

"Albion Yard, tomorrow, 9 p.m."

Ben grabbed the phone. "Hang on, can we make it Friday…?"

Hugo interrupted, softly, firmly. "Tomorrow. If you need to be there, you will be there."

The line went dead, and we were in our glass box, gazing out across the empty car park. On one side the derelict terrace was a cut-out of darkness. On the other, the backs of the precinct rose sheer as a fortress, and there could have been eyes on every ledge, in every alley, watching. Shadows spilled across the tarmac and I had the crazy thought that if one of them touched us it would stick and cling; we'd be like seabirds in an oil-slick, flapping feebly, being choked of light and air.

A cat came like a slingshot out from beneath the dumped car, and I saw the mouse freeze beneath its paws. The cat lifted a paw and whacked its prey head over heels, a small slash of the claws, enough to maim but not to kill. Just playing. Suddenly it looked up at the phone booth, one paw raised. Its eyes, wide and black for night-hunting, stared straight at us, as if it somehow *knew*.

6

"You promised!" Dee hissed.

"I know, I know," Ben said. "I'm sorry. The film's on all week. Let's go Friday."

"What's wrong with tonight?"

I'd come round the corner of the Rat Run, bound for Ben's house, and before I could duck back out of sight or say "Hi", there they were, at the door. They were deep in a quarrel and didn't look up or notice me.

"I just ... just don't feel like it," Ben squirmed. "With the gig tomorrow and all that. We'll enjoy it more on Friday."

"OK," said Dee. "I'll come round anyway."

"No..." said Ben. "The thing is..."

Dee went rigid. "Ben Davies, you're a pathetic liar. You're going out, aren't you? Where? Who with?"

"Emod!" Just in time, Ben noticed me. "Just the bloke. I'm going out with Emod. Got to see this guy about an amp," Ben said too loudly. "That's right, isn't it, Emod?"

There was a very long moment as Dee looked from Ben, to me, to Ben and back to me.

"Oh … yeah," I said faintly. Dee's eyes seemed to get bigger than ever. Hurt, betrayed. Then she turned on her heel and slung off, not quite running. The lanes swallowed the sound of her feet.

Albion Yard was nothing you could call a street. Tucked in at the back of the precinct, it was a loading bay where lorries backed in and out all day, with warning lights flashing and beeping, for several department stores. Now it was empty, a small concrete canyon with a sign, NO PUBLIC RIGHT OF WAY. One thing was obvious: no one could possibly live here.

Ben squinted into the half-dark and drizzle. "Are you sure that's where he said?" I nodded. He frowned. "He could have been putting us on. Maybe we didn't say the right thing."

"He could have just put the phone down. Why bother to bring us here?"

"Hey, you don't think he guessed, do you? About us and Alia? I mean, the other things he said … how did he *know*?"

There was a scuffle in the corner; a pile of cardboard pizza cartons shuddered and slid. A long shape twitched out, stopped with a jolt and balanced on its hind legs, sniffing. Rat. One look at us, it was off.

"Look," I said. "This is stupid. He's not here. Let's split."

"I want to have a good look first," said Ben. Albion Yard was a dead end: concrete walls, without windows mostly, going three or four storeys up on all sides. I could still see one orange streetlamp behind us in the street but looking at it just made the shadows seem darker. Our footsteps rattled back off walls and metal: wide steel shutters marked with WORLD OF TOYS or UNCLE LUIGI'S PIZZA had been rolled down and padlocked in place.

There was a faint hum. Over our heads there was the zigzag of a fire-escape. The monk's-cowl of a ventilation duct bent down towards us with its warm stale breath.

"OK, OK," Ben said. "Let's get out of here." That's when I saw it, matt black, scratched and heavy and not new: the motorbike. "Hold it…" I said. And that's when Hugo's voice spoke to us out of nowhere, echoing between the blank walls, hanging in the air.

"You came," it said. There was a slight metallic ring to it I couldn't place. "Did your parents never tell you it's not safe to walk the streets by night?" He laughed quietly, and there was a shudder of wings as a small flock of starlings peeled from their roosts on high ledges, beat round above us and landed again.

"Where are you?" Ben said into nowhere. "What's it all about?"

"I needed to know if you were serious, or if you were just playing. Were you afraid?"

"We don't like being messed about," said Ben.

"Good, good," the hollow voice chuckled. "I like your spirit…"

"There!" I whispered. "Look." Of course, the voice was coming down the ventilation shaft, though where the man actually was, who knows?

"Enough of these games," the voice said. "It's time we met … in the flesh." There was a clash of metal high above us, and a cloud of starlings broke and scattered, beating round and round above us with a hissing squealing sound. As they settled back gradually, I heard the mechanical whirr, and I spotted the movement. In the middle of the criss-cross of the fire-escape, a small metal lift-cage came down, very slowly, as if it was winching down a very heavy weight, and we waited at the bottom, staring up, with the drizzle soaking into our backs and hair.

Clunk. The lift-cage shuddered and was on the ground. The diamond-shaped slats of the folding door did not clash open. It was empty, we saw at a glance. We were meant to get in.

"Hold it," I said. "That isn't a passenger lift, it's just a hoist…"

"Do you want to see this guy or not?" Ben whispered. "You stay here if you like." And he slid the door open.

"OK," I said, "count me in."

It wasn't quite big enough to stand upright, and

though the floor was a square of battered iron all the walls were bars. No sooner had Ben concertina'd the door shut than there was a deep *clunk* and the whole thing shuddered. It groaned, swayed and lifted off. A coil of greasy cable started looping down beside us and the zigzag girders of the fire-escape slid slowly past, first one side, then the other. I shrank into the middle of the floor space. I could see much too clearly in my mind's eye what would happen if I poked a finger through the bars.

The canyon of Albion Yard was sinking into the dark beneath us. Over the roofs of the precinct we could see the dull glow of city night sky. We had climbed two storeys, three... We were going to the top. Then, *clunk* again, the winding stopped.

We weren't on a landing. Outside the door there was space, and a long drop to Albion Yard. "Hey!" Ben called, and the lift-cage wobbled. All around us, starlings ruffled on the ledges, testing their wings, their sharp beaks opening in that snake-hiss sound.

Then there was Hugo, outside the door where there was nothing, looming at the lift door, looking in. Just looking. I waited for that stony face to break into something: laughter, anger, anything... It didn't. "Well..." he said in that level voice. "Two birds in a cage..."

"Very funny." Ben had gritted his teeth. "Now let us out."

"I'm not keeping you," said Hugo. "Just open the door and you're free."

I tried the handle. It clicked easily. Not locked. I slid it open, just enough to see. There was a narrow ledge where Hugo was standing, balanced easily above a sickening drop. It was only a girder's width. Between it and the lift door was a gap.

"Just a step," he said. "On the ground, you wouldn't think twice. You see? It's only fear that keeps you in your cage."

"Why should we?" Ben said.

"No reason at all. Except there is something I can teach you ... and you don't know what. If you want to go back, just say the word."

Ben swore under his breath, but he moved to the door of the lift-cage. "Don't," I said, but it was too late. He braced himself and made the step. As he pushed off the cage swung back and clanged into the girders behind it, and I staggered, as starlings panicked off their perches, wheeling up into the twilight with a thud of wing-beats and a pressure-cooker hiss. When I looked up, Ben was upright on the ledge, with one hand braced on an iron upright. "It's OK," he said, reaching the other towards me. His palm was sweaty and cold when I took it, but then there was no going back. "Come on," he whispered. "Show him!" So I stepped.

For a moment it felt that the cage stayed still behind me and the fire-escape swayed. The cloud of starlings swirled back in beneath me. "Good," said Hugo, a metre or so away. "Now, keep your eyes on me. Come, join me in my eyrie."

Then we were sitting by him on a wide ledge, just under the rooftops of the precinct, and there was half of Borsley laid out at our feet: the empty car park, the roofs of the Arcana café, and dreary streets and streets beyond. Up here, though, was different. There was a buzz in the air, a kind of throbbing, and it was a minute before I realized it was my heartbeat and blood in my veins. It didn't make sense but I couldn't help smiling. "Wow," I said. "Is that what you mean about *flying*?" And I bit my tongue.

Ben was looking at me. So was Hugo. "I mean…" I stumbled. "I don't mean you, I mean, people say that, don't they?" Hugo grinned again, but not like you grin at a joke. His teeth, I could see, were long, uneven, stained with grey.

"Don't waste our time pretending," he said. "I know who you are. Alia thought you might come in the end."

"Then why didn't she tell us," said Ben. "If she'd just *said*…"

"In a primitive tribe…" he said. "No, it's foolish to say *primitive*. In any ancient culture that has stood the test of time, they know that wisdom, adulthood even, does not just happen. It has to be gained. There are always tests. Ordeals. Initiations. And for those who will grow to be shamans…"

"Shamans?" Ben said. "Alia always used to talk about that kind of stuff…"

"Did Alia tell you?" Hugo cut in sharply.

"No, no. She used to talk about all sorts. It's all

these books she reads." *Used to…* Ben was right. She didn't prattle on about her wild ideas any more. Like lots of things these days, she kept it to herself.

"Good." Hugo relaxed. "And even if she had told you before tonight, would you have understood?" He waited for us not to answer. "This," he said, "is only the beginning. This was just a game. Come with me." His eyes were deep-set, full of shadow. Then they fixed on me and I couldn't look away.

"Where?" Ben said.

"The group," said Hugo, "meets not far from here. We have members at various stages of … progress, shall we say. Your friend Alia is one of my most gifted pupils."

"And … and if we don't come?" I said faintly. For some reason I thought of the rat, on its scavenging business, three storeys down beneath our feet. If we were to … slip, Ben and I, it would be several hours before the early-morning lorries backed into the yard and found us. We'd told no one we were coming here, of course. Only Hugo and the rat need ever know.

As if he saw this in my mind, he gave that long-toothed smile. "If you don't come?" he said to Ben. "Then you will be an ordinary young man, in an ordinary rock band. Only, unlike most of them, you will know to the end of your days how hopelessly ordinary you are. And how you threw away your chance … to fly. And you?" He meant me. "You'll tinker with your electrical gadgets till the day you die. An oddball. The sad old geezer parents tell their children not to talk to. A fate worse than death, no?" He glanced over the edge, to the rat's patch. "And what all this means…" He swept his hand out over Borsley. "What all this means, you'll never know."

7

There were a few rungs of an iron ladder, then we stepped on to a concrete plateau. It was wide and flat and square, with pyramidal mountains here and there, or a softly glowing dome, or geometric valleys, like a construct out of cyberspace. Beyond the straight edge there was sky, like the end of the world. It was another world … but it was Borsley. We were walking on the flat roofs of the shopping mall.

Hugo let us stare. He watched us, noting our reactions, as if this was all just part of some experiment. "Wait a mo," I said. "All this talk about power … all these promises…" Now we weren't on that dizzying edge any more, I felt bolder. "What's in it for you?"

"There aren't many of us," he said. "When I recognize a kindred spirit…"

"This group of yours…" Ben joined in. "You haven't told us what it costs."

Hugo nodded, very slowly. "There is no money involved, if that's what you mean."

"Then … what *is?*" I said.

He opened both his hands, big strangler's hands, palms upwards. "If you knew that," he said, "there would be no risk. It would just be a bargain like…" He gestured at the mall beneath us. "Like them down there."

Around us there were ventilation ducts like giant beehives, buzzing slightly, and aerials and satellite bowls and wrist-thick snakes of coiling wires. At the edge of the shallow dome I peered in. It was tinted perspex, speckled with rain, and I realized with a lurch that I was looking down the light-well into the central concourse with its escalators and its fountains and its hanging gardens and lights that stayed on dimly, for security reasons, through the night.

Security… Just a few hours ago the mall had been an antheap, hundreds of people busying about their late-night shopping. How would they look, seen from the hawk's, the predator's eye-view? Scurrying mice and insects, busy in their little world, quite unaware… Meanwhile the night-people, Hugo and whoever, could be looking down on them from here.

He was right by my shoulder; I could smell the raw leather of his coat. "Thousands of them, think of it, gazing into windows full of TVs, videos, all the things they long for. Led by the nose. And they never look up. *If you want privacy, pitch your tent in the market place.* Tibetan proverb. Oh, yes, you can depend on people not to notice what they wouldn't understand. Ordinary people, that is."

There was a whiff of that bitter-sharp incense somewhere nearby as Hugo led us back towards the little block that must have housed the winding-gear. Propped up against it on one side was a kind of shanty shack, with no windows and a tarpaulin draped across one side for a door. On this concrete plateau in the sky, it was a nomad's tent.

"Do they know?" said Ben. "The security people, I mean. The caretaker…"

"I *am* the caretaker." Hugo grinned, and parted the heavy flap of the waterproof curtain. He bent almost double to enter, and a wave of incense hit us as we followed.

There was a candle burning in there and at first that was all I could see. The flame shuddered with the draught that came in with us, and the shadows swayed, but the shapes of people sitting cross-legged stayed straight-backed, upright and perfectly still. As Hugo motioned us to our places in the circle, the candle picked out faces one by one.

There was the Beansprout from the café. His colourless eyes glanced sideways at us but he did not move or speak. In the half-light his wispy beard and hair looked white, as if he'd aged fifty years since we saw him. There was a rat-faced little man beside him, whom I seemed to recognize. Yes, he worked in the library, nothing high up, and I don't think he liked his job much. Once I asked him a question about capacitors and he told me to go and look it up in a book.

There was a middle-aged woman with a tight straight mouth. She sat painfully upright, quivering with the effort, as if something inside her could snap any moment. There was an old man with two tufts of white hair above his ears and a faraway look, like dotty vicars in old films. And there was Alia, in profile, staring at the flame. Her cheeks were very pale, with a slight sheen as if she was sweating. It could have been a wax effigy of her, she was so still, except two points of flame glinted in her eyes, which did not blink. She didn't look up to greet us, but I knew she knew.

Candle-light does things to eyes. I saw this programme once that explained about candle-lit dinners and the romance thing. It makes your pupils go large, so it looks as if you fancy each other. As simple as that. There was something about Alia's eyes, or the shadowy space where her eyes must have been – something fierce and cold and burning, and that glint inside them. I knew we mustn't speak to her. She'd shrivel us to cinders, one breath out of place.

Without a word, Hugo reached out and clicked a switch. A cassette player. So the nomad's tent had mod cons after all.

It started with a drum beat, very soft and low on the threshold of hearing. It rattled my eardrums like a moth, a huge moth ghosting in out of the darkness as if it wants to come in, bumping and scratching at the window pane. This went on, getting louder very slowly, then there was a jangling with it that made me think of the pitbull they keep tethered in the back yard next door, pacing to and fro and tugging at its chain. Then the voice came in. I say *came in*, because it seemed to come from outside. I don't mean outside the shack, I mean outside this world. At first I didn't guess it was a human voice at all.

It was deep in the belly, like another animal in there, swallowed whole and growling. There were other notes in it as well, a whining high up in the head, a dentist's drill or a metal mosquito. There was more than one voice in it, as if we'd opened a door into a hidden room, where there was a fierce old man grumbling, casting curses maybe, and a toddler whimpering with fright, and the rattling throat-sound of someone fighting for his final breath. If there were words, they were no language I could guess at, maybe no earthly language at all.

Hugo clicked off the tape abruptly. "A rare recording," he said. "A throat-singer of the Kekyut tribe of western Siberia."

The librarian looked up. "Overtone chanting," he said, "similar to the monks of…"

"We all know about the techniques," Hugo cut in. The man shut up at once. "More to the point," said

Hugo, "among the Kekyuts it is strictly forbidden for the uninitiated to listen to a shaman's trance song. Punishable, in fact, by death. It took a brave man to make this recording." He paused. "The next year's expedition found the cassette in his tent. The wolves, they said, had disposed of everything except the bones. But before we go on..." He turned to Ben and me and smiled. "Let's welcome two new enquiring spirits. Ben and..."

"Emod," I said.

"Emod, yes." As my eyes became used to the gloom, it was starting to dawn on me just how cramped we were. The walls were draped with heavy hangings, some with an Indian feel like the Kunalini in the café, some with jagged abstract patterns in which there were hints of animals or birds in flight. The shack had looked small on the outside; on the inside it was smaller, and with no windows or door and this throat-stinging incense burning, I imagined the last of the air being lapped up by the candle, so we couldn't breathe at all.

"The shaman's song," said Hugo, "is in spirit speech, the language he hears when he enters the spirit world. The ritual is as usual. After days of fasting and chanting, the shaman enters a trance, and watches his own death." He looked at Ben and me. "The death of the body, that is. He sees himself eaten by foxes and his eyes pecked out by ravens. Finally the white owl comes, the Arctic owl, the owl of death, and picks apart the bones." He leaned forward and touched the flame with something grey. It sizzled and a puff of sharp smoke stung my nostrils. For a moment the floor seemed to drop out beneath me; I was in the Green Room, with that smell, and the feather. Alia's feather. The grey owl of death. I blinked – keep a hold on yourself, Emod – and I was back in Hugo's shack and listening as his voice went on.

"When all the bones are clean and dry, and only then, can the shaman's spirit spread its wings and fly. He can enter the world of the spirit creatures. Or he can transform himself. He can move as a dog or a snake or a bird. He has power."

The tight-lipped woman looked up sharply. "This power…" she said. "Would the shaman use it … say, if someone had angered them? If someone had hurt you deeply, could you use this power then?"

"Real power," said Hugo quietly, "is nothing to do with right and wrong. If you have it, you know."

I glanced at Alia. She had not moved. Her hair was swept back, her face straining forward, very pale, like someone walking head on into a cold wind. Who was this girl? Six months ago she'd been a shy kid with a nervous laugh and puppy fat. Somehow she'd been stripped of both things, stripped down to essentials. Yes, transformed. For a moment in the candle-light I thought I could see how her face might look at a hundred years old.

Thrummm… Hugo had reached behind him and picked something off the wall. It was wide, round, almost flat with a taut parchment skin. He caught my look. "Not Kekyut," he said. "Another tribe, probably extinct now. Still, a very sacred object. A real shaman's drum." He stroked it lightly with his fingertips, and that low rattling *thrummm*, like in the music, filled the room. The rhythm was very slow at first, and not loud, but I felt it in my bones.

"Now we chant."

"I can't sing," I said.

"Forget singing," said Hugo. "Listen," and he let his breath out in a hissing sigh. The next had a faint *aaaah!* in it, then a growling, droning hum. In the small cramped space, the big man's voice set up a resonance. "The voice knows what to do," he said, as the *thrummm* of the drum picked up a beat. A heartbeat. "Let it free." Hugo's eyes closed, his lips parted slightly and a voice came through them, nothing like his own. It was ragged, deep and breathy, rattling deep in the cave of his ribs. The pant of an animal, hunting or hunted. Cornered, in pain, speared, broken, bleeding, can't escape, can't die... And it went on and on.

Hugo closed his eyes, and his face was a carving. I glanced at Ben, but he had forgotten me. He was watching Alia, as she picked up the rhythm of the breathing, tilting her head back and letting the first sounds come. Then it was all around me, the others were picking it up, like a complex machine with different cogwheels engaging with the main drive one by one. Then somehow it was inside me too: I could feel all the breathing, in, out, pulsing, driving, lifting me and carrying me along. I'm not going to join in this game, I remember thinking. Ben could make a fool of himself if he liked, I thought, but me...

I couldn't say when I stopped thinking. It's like trying to spot the moment when you fall asleep. I was bored for a time, quite a long time, then I wasn't. All I know is that it went on, went on, went on with the voices building sometimes, sometimes ebbing, till I wondered if these people ever had to breathe. I kept having to gasp an extra breath just to keep in the rhythm, and there were little sparks of light in the shadows that I thought at first were chinks from outside, till I realized it was me. All those bodies, too close: I was hot. But it wasn't unpleasant, floating on those voices. They were round me and inside me, like a tingling in the bones.

I remember staring at the drum and seeing the patterns on it very clearly, more clearly than I normally see things at all. They were stick figures, really, quite childish. I can draw better than that, I thought, and I can't draw at all. They were cartoons, but there wasn't a story. There were deer with antlers much bigger than they were, and a thing with tusks that might have been a walrus, and stick people walking, hunting, fighting, standing round. One of them was lying down, coming apart, and there was a half-human winged thing hovering above his bones.

A circuit diagram, came a stray thought from

nowhere. That's what it looks like. Little symbols for transistors, capacitors, what have you. Most people couldn't make sense of one, but I could. I wondered if Hugo could read shaman-signs like that. Like a map. I thought I might shift then, and I tried to move but couldn't quite make contact with my hands or feet.

Then there was a jolt and I was falling. No, not falling: I was high up, looking down, swaying with vertigo like when I'd sat with Hugo, on the ledge he called his eyrie, but higher than that, much higher. I grabbed for a handhold and clung on as the whole of Borsley spread out beneath me, glowing in the dark. It wasn't just light. There were spider-web filaments binding one house to the next, sometimes braiding into thick ropes like cables in ducts under the street. It was energy, not just electric but all kinds, in a massive circuit diagram with every connection marked in. It was power.

But the web was alive. As I steadied my breathing, on the edge of panic, I could see little sparks run down the lines, red glows of overheating, even a smell of scorching. Someone ought to warn them, I thought, before the circuit overloads... There were figures on the ledge beside me. As I looked a brown rat sat up on its tail and twitched its whiskers. A scrawny grey pigeon was pecking, pecking at a tiny piece of seed between its feet. A lean cat crouched low, and its tail began to thrash. I froze. Was it looking at me? What was I? I turned the other way and there was the great bird, whitish-grey, half hawk, half owl, with its huge eyes on me.

There was a splutter of sparks beneath me: the circuit had blown. A whole block went black and burst into a reddish smudge of smoke, right near the centre of the map. There was a thin mingled hissing, almost too high for the ear to hear, that started like the starlings but turned into human voices wailing, far below. Then there were lower whoops and wails: fire engines and ambulances, red lights and blue lights flashing as the precinct started going up in flames. Then the scream was all around me, not human any more. The grey bird opened its billhook beak as it smelt burnt flesh, it shrieked like the voice of its victims and I staggered as it swooped towards me, its wing brushed my face and it wheeled out in the smoke that rose around us through the night. I was grabbing at handholds, missing, and the bird's shriek was my own cry as I teetered on the edge, then fell.

I was lying on concrete. Ben was dragging me out of the shack, and someone was groaning; I think it was me. "Fire..." I tried to warn them. Ben was shaking his head. True, there was no smoke, no sirens. The people from the group stood round staring. "Don't worry, he's fainted, that's all," Ben said, but I could see there was something else in their eyes as they looked at me. Only Hugo seemed perfectly calm. He was watching me intently, from a distance, nodding slightly. There might even have been a slight smile on his face.

"You OK?" Ben said. "Don't *do* that!"

"Don't do what?"

Then Alia was bending over me. "Emod," she whispered. "What happened? Tell me."

"Nothing," I said. In my mind I heard the screams, I smelt the burning. No, don't think… I took a deep breath. "Nothing *happened*," I said.

"That's not true," she said. "What did you see?"

I shook my head. It hurt. I got to my feet but the ground wasn't steady. They manhandled me to the lift, and Ben climbed in beside me. "Hey, Alia," he said as Hugo's hand went to the switch. "We've got to talk about tomorrow. The gig… Aren't you coming?"

Alia shook her head. "But…" Ben said. *Clunk*: the cable started winding.

"I said, trust me," she said as we sank out of sight. "It'll be great, just you see."

8

"She's doing it again!" Clive was pacing like a caged thing. "I mean: once you can understand, but if she thinks she can do this to us every gig … I'm not going to stand for it. It does my head in. Hey…" he said weakly. "She *is* going to turn up, isn't she?"

"Of course," said Ben. But he kept on glancing at the door. It was zero minus five minutes, and Alia wasn't there.

The Hot Spot Club was all Borsley had for nightlife if you were under twenty-five and could pass as seventeen. It was on the first floor, over the gas showroom, with most of the windows painted over so they flickered red, blue, green when there were flashing lights inside. No one went to the precinct by night, so they could make a bit of noise without neighbours complaining. It was just a disco most nights, with a fat guy mumbling at a couple of turntables, but if you wanted the scene in Borsley, that was where you went. I didn't much.

"It was that rehearsal, wasn't it?" said Clive. "What a cock-up. Has anybody seen her since then? Like, at school?" He looked at Dee. She shrugged. "I may have," she said, off-hand. "Don't know where she gets to these days. She doesn't have lunch any more." She stalked off for the fifteenth time to check the door.

Ben leaned over to me. "It's because of last night, isn't it?"

"What's that?" Clive said sharply. "Last night? You been having special practices, then? Without me? Did you hear that, Geek?"

"No," said Ben. "We just saw her in town, that's all."

"Oh, yeah? And you just didn't mention it. There's too many secrets in this band, if you ask me."

"What do you mean...?" Ben started, but the door burst open. There was Alia, in black, with a black cloak flapping as she swept right past. Her face was pale and rigid. Either she was furious, or she was about to cry. Without a word, she vanished backstage. Just behind came Dee.

"What's up?" said Ben. "What did you say to her?"

Dee sighed. "It wasn't me. It was Natalie, Tracy, that lot, bunch of girls from our school, and they've got these stupid boyfriends with them so they're

73

showing off. They never liked Alia much..." She shrugged. "They were just laughing, not quite saying anything, just being bitchy, you know, the way girls do."

"What did Alia do?"

"Nothing," said Dee. "That was what was weird. Usually at school she'd give them an answer, something clever, even if she was really hurt inside. But she didn't say anything. She just went all … hard."

"Then go and calm her down," said Clive. "We're meant to be on. Now."

"Sorry, not me." Dee shook her head. Ben got to his feet. "I should have guessed *you* would," Dee snapped.

"I'll go and see what's happening," I said.

Alia didn't move as I came up behind her, but she heard me. She was waiting, ready to walk on stage. "Where are the others?" she said without expression. "The DJ's getting worried."

"We … *we* were worried," I said. "Are you all right?"

"We're meant to be on," she said with a quiver in her voice. "Tell the others I'm waiting."

"OK," I said. "OK, you're the boss."

It must have been the article about the band in Contax that did it: the Hot Spot was full. It was a mixed crowd, not just their usual, with kids coming in from outside Borsley because they'd heard the buzz. There were all kinds of styles, too: a bunch of

74

black leather in one corner, a clump of neo-hippies over there, some rave types, and some crusties in their combat gear, looking as if they'd just stepped off a convoy. There were local kids too, the Traceys and Natalies and their boyfriends, who'd just called by to see what the fuss was about. Most of them turned up with six-packs in their hands. It was a volatile mix, and the DJ didn't know what to play. No wonder he wanted the band on, fast. He glanced up with relief as they walked on.

"Here we go, kids." He cut the music. "You've read about them in the papers. Contax thinks they're the greatest thing since sliced bread. Can't say I'd heard about them till last month, but I've got it on good authority that you're in for something special, so put your hands together and give them a welcome. Transformer!" He shut off his smile and scuttled out of sight.

I don't know how Alia did it. As far as I could see, she just walked out and stood there, maybe slower than usual, or the way she looked at them, with no expression on her face, no half-apologetic smile. There were a few scattered whistles and joke cheers from the kids who'd teased her, but she turned that look their way, very slowly, and they shuffled, then were quiet. She let the silence last. And last. I could see Ben quivering with the tension but he couldn't move. Then Alia turned her head, very slightly, and nodded and the others came to life as if she'd thrown a switch. Geek usually likes a good *One* ...

two … *three* … but they went in bang on cue, like stepping off a cliff. And they flew.

"Look at her…" Dee muttered beside me. Alia reached forward to the mike, the black cape slipped off her shoulders and crumpled like black foam around her feet. She was in black from her neck to her feet, very tight and straight-down, but her arms were thin and pale and bare. Already the rest of her, in the black, was somehow not quite there. "I mean, look at her!" Dee said again. "Who does she think she is?" I don't think I answered. I was watching Alia's fingers, clutching the mike so hard that sharp knuckles stood out. If she lost her grip, I remember thinking, she'd be swept away.

I don't know much about what happened in the first few songs. I don't know if Alia was singing well. Once or twice Dee made a little hiss when Alia went for a high note, so I guess it wasn't perfect, but it was something else better than that. It sounded dangerous. Sometimes she sounded as if it really hurt, sometimes as if she'd hurt *you* if you got too close.

It was nothing like the rehearsal. Ben's solos, for one thing … Alia didn't take her eyes off him while he played. Now, Ben's a good musician, in the way that music teachers see it, but he'd be the first to admit that he doesn't go *wild*. He doesn't let go. Now all of a sudden he was going for it, pigtail flying, fingers scuttling up the fretboard higher than I thought they were ever meant to go. When

the next verse came round he was still up there looping the loop, and Alia caught Clive's eye and nodded, and they took it round again and again till Ben found his way back to earth. There was cheering like a good wave breaking on a surfing beach.

Before it died Alia brought up her arms above her head. *Clap – clap – clap...* She nodded to the lights man at the back of the hall, not a word said but he understood. The flashing coloured lights went off, and there was only the white spot on the band, and the FIRE EXIT sign on the door. The crowd was a sea of shadow, washing to and fro. Their clapping caught her rhythm, then her foot was stamping and the crowd was stamping with her till the rafters shook. I thought of those stories about how armies have to break step when they march across a bridge, and though this place was concrete I could have sworn I felt it move. *Thud – thud – thud...* Alia gave a nod to Clive and he joined in, one note blending with the stamping in a single pulse. Ben was slapping his strings on the pick-ups with a whiplash sound, not quite a note. Alia nodded to Geek but Geek wasn't having it. This hadn't been in the rehearsal. Geek had had enough. He put down his sticks and crossed his arms.

Before he could stop her Alia had grabbed the nearest snare drum and was stroking it, crooked in her elbow just like Hugo held the shaman drum. The same beat: *thrumm ... thrumm...* A heartbeat at first, then faster. I couldn't see how she was doing it, but it was her, all right, pushing the pulse of it faster, but so gradually you didn't know. All I could see was the crowd, which had been swaying steadily in one beat with each other, start to break up, with side-ripples spreading out, bouncing back from the walls, colliding with the main sway in a jostle, good-tempered at first, then harder, so people started to call, "Hey, watch it…" and to push back. At the same time Alia started on the chant.

It was deep in her stomach at first, like the first flutter of feedback on Clive's bass amp. There was a whine in it too, like the shaman singer from the night before. It was hypnotic, almost soothing as it rode the beat, but at the same time it began to set your teeth on edge. One or two voices joined in, then others; there wasn't a note exactly but they merged together in a steady grating drone.

Near the front there was a scuffle, as one of the motorbike kids lost his footing. His mates caught him and in one movement threw him upright and he lashed out at random, sending Natalie's bloke reeling back, blood gushing from his nose. Alia bent close to the mike, with a long breath drawn in slowly, sighing, rattling in her throat. Then she screamed.

The spotlight went off like a flashbulb, fixing everybody in an after-image of shouting faces, fists raised, elbows hacking. Then it was black, and kids were screaming as the fight began. It might have been the lighting man who reached for the switch, but just for a moment the red light strobed weakly, then fluttered and died. It was enough, though: someone shouted, "Fire!"

Then they were jammed in the door, shrieking and struggling. Someone picked up a stool and hurled it at a window. There was a shatter and a gash of streetlight poured in, to show a girl, and it might have been Tracey, crumpling in the splinters, wailing. The jam at the door gave way and the crowd was tumbling downstairs, some of them shouting and scuffling as they burst on to the street.

The police were there in minutes, I'll give them that. A shop window or two had gone, and some of the kids were dipping into the goodies as the shrill of alarms mixed with the nee-naw of the squad cars. Most of the crowd broke ranks at that point, some of them standing there blankly, shell-shocked, some of them scattering round the precinct leaving just the echo of their running feet.

When the lights came back on, Ben was with the manager already, then Clive and Dee were with them, jabbering, gesturing, faces white and stunned. As far as I could see, we'd lost our drummer. Geek had gone. Alia stood exactly where I'd seen her last, before the riot. Slowly, she turned and bent down to gather her cloak from the floor.

"Alia…" I whispered.

"Leave it," she said without looking up.

"But Alia…! What happened?" She straightened

up and for a moment I thought she was going to blast me. As usual, I was wrong.

"Emod…" She rested her hand on my arm. "Help me." I stared at her. "Get Ben off my back," she said.

"Don't … don't you like him?"

"Of course I do. You know all the girls fancy him, but…" Her voice dropped. "It's more important than that for me."

"You mean the band?"

"Not just that. Emod, you know what I was like. I bet Dee told you. Shy and fat and ugly, that's what they all said." I was shaking my head. She didn't notice. "But it's going to be different now. It's started happening." Her hand had tightened on my arm, thin fingers digging into my skin like claws. "I'm never going back to all that, never. I'd rather die." The grip relaxed. "Hugo is helping me. Emod, don't let Ben interfere."

"But … he's worried, that's all. In case Hugo has … some kind of hold over you."

To my surprise, she smiled. "Oh no," she said calmly. "No hold. Look, I don't expect anyone to understand. Just … please don't let Ben get too close. I'm afraid."

"What, of Hugo…?"

"No!" She looked away. "Of what I might do." At the back of the hall the police were with the others, heads were shaking, shoulders shrugged in *search me* gestures as they scanned the wreckage. "I mean, if I'd been *really* angry, I don't know what would have happened."

I winced. "I think I do."

There was a long pause, as her eyes met mine. Not a word spoken, but... She nodded very slightly. *We're in this together, then?* it seemed to say. With a shiver, she whipped her cloak around her shoulders. "Don't tell anyone what I've just said. Not Ben. Not Dee. It would only make things worse. Promise?" The full force of her eyes was on me, and I bowed my head.

No! I knew I should say. *Count me out.* But I didn't. I only half wanted to. Instead, I looked up into that fierce hunter's stare of hers and said, "OK."

9

"**B**en!" I stepped out from behind the Coke machine, and he jumped. I'd been lying in wait for him all lunchtime in his usual places. Now here he was scuttling down the corridor as if… "Are you avoiding me?"

"Course not," he muttered, glancing round. "Look, I've had people on my back all morning. Everybody's heard about the club…"

"Fame," I said. "Isn't that what you wanted?" He gave a twisted sort of smile.

"We've got to talk," I said.

He glanced round again. "OK. Not here." He didn't unwind until we were in the furthest corner of the canteen. Most people were back at classes, like I should have been, and the place was nearly empty. "I was going to talk to you…" Ben stared into the coffee that he hadn't touched. A thin scum of powdered milk had risen to the surface and was swirling very slowly like a spiral nebula. "I just needed to get one or two things straightened out first."

"Things?"

"I'll explain," he said. "Later."

I couldn't take much more of this. A lunch hour is only so long. "Where were you last night?" I said. "You aren't in college all day, so I call round to see if you're ill. You're out."

"You're starting to sound like my mother. Hell, Emod, you're starting to sound like Dee."

"That's another thing..."

"Don't start on that. Leave Dee out of this, OK?"

"OK, OK ... so where were you?" I said. He looked at the floor and didn't answer. "You were out with *her*, weren't you?"

"Who?"

"Oh, come off it..." This was incredible. I've seen little kids with their parents like this, not quite telling lies, just seeing how little of the truth they can get away with. This was Ben, my best friend... "Alia, of course."

He nodded. "It isn't like you think," he said quickly. "I'm not *going out* with Alia. It's nothing like that. It's ... it's more important."

"Great. What do I tell Dee then? Ben and Alia... He's not *going out* with her. Not love and sex. No, it's *more important*!" And where had I heard that line before, anyway? I remembered. Alia.

"Look, forget Dee. I'll tell her … when she's ready."

Sometimes, when a bulb's about to blow, you get a high-pitched whine. At first it's so high you can't hear it, and as it gets louder you still don't notice because it's been there all the time. Then suddenly it's like a corkscrew in your ear. That's how it felt now, in the canteen, trying to listen calmly to Ben. There was a whine in my head that told me: something's going to blow.

"Hugo," I said. "It's something to do with him, isn't it?"

"I was just getting round to that," Ben muttered. "If you'd give me a chance."

"I'm listening." And out it came. The plan. Yes, he'd phoned Hugo. He'd tried Alia first. After the riot at the club he just wanted to make sure she was all right. She'd seemed so calm on the night, he said, he thought it might be shock. She was out, her parents weren't sure where. So it had to be Hugo.

There was a moment's pause on the phone, then Hugo said, "It's time for us to talk. Meet me at the Arcana." When Ben got there, Alia was waiting too.

"The thing you've got to understand about Hugo," Ben said, looking up from his coffee, "is that he's not doing any of this for himself. He doesn't even charge for his classes. OK, people give him money, but that's because they want to. He just leaves a bowl out. He'd do the classes anyway, because he believes in the stuff."

"Do you?" I said.

Ben frowned and shrugged, as if it was a pesky question. "The point is, he can help us with the band."

"Him? Hugo?!"

"Don't laugh. He used to sing himself…"

"When? In the 1920s?"

"Sixties, I should think. But then he got into the chanting and the whole spiritual thing. The point is…" he said again, before I could interrupt, "he's still got contacts. He can get us places."

"Oh, yeah?"

"He knows Jed Alexander."

I was downing the dregs of my coffee when he said it, and I choked. Jed Alexander is big. It's not so much the hits he had, though he still turns up at Live Aid gigs like a real star; he's a record label these days, and of course the Whole World Festival. There are bands from all over the world, the stranger the better; there are *kora* players from Mali, didgeridoo masters from the Australian outback, devil-dancers from Bali, you name it…

"He might be able to get us a spot at the festival."

I gaped.

"Just a small spot," he said. "Not top billing. But Jed Alexander will be there. He'll hear us, that's the big thing. If he likes us, well…" Ben looked up at me for the first time and his eyes were bright.

"Wow," I said. I'd been coming to terms with the thought that Transformer were going to go down as the biggest disaster in history. I'd just about managed it, and now … this. "Wh-when?" I said.

"Couple of weeks. The 25th."

The date rang a bell. A warning bell. "Aren't you forgetting something? Your exam…"

There was a pause. "I know," Ben said. "I've thought about it. But … the Whole World Festival … Emod, this could be *it*!"

"What about Alia? Her parents might not let her."

"Come on, you've seen them. She can wind them round her little finger."

"What about Clive?" I was playing for time. "And Geek?"

"Ah…" Ben's forehead wrinkled. "Thing is, Geek's left."

Great. First he tells me we've got our big break. Then he tells me this… "Oh, brilliant," I said. "Clive won't play without him. That's the end of the band."

"No, Emod," Ben said quietly. "It's just the beginning. Clive won't leave, not if there's a chance of meeting Jed Alexander."

"But the drums…"

"You're the technical wiz. Just wire us up a drum machine. Simple. Geek was no great shakes… Hey, you've said it yourself. You said the only difference between Geek and a beat box was beat boxes don't get drunk. What's the problem?"

"It's … it's Hugo…"

"We always said we could do with a manager. Now we've got one for free."

"Hugo's our manager now, is he?" Ben didn't need to answer. It had been closing in around us gradually. Suddenly there it was in place – click! – like a cage door shutting; we were inside and we weren't even struggling. Not even surprised. *Of course*, that's all I thought. It was as if Hugo had been our manager, secretly, for quite some time – before we even met him, maybe?

"Ben, think … what happened at the club…"

Ben looked puzzled. "What do you mean? So we had a bad crowd. A power cut. Bad luck. Forget about it." Ben was leaning forward, almost pleading. "You'll do it, won't you? Emod, after all we've been through, you won't let us down?"

I suppose that was the moment I could have said no. I thought about it afterwards, the way you go back over and write the scripts of things you never said. I could have said: *Ben, this is getting weird and crazy. Count me out.* I could have stood up and made for the door.

And if I had, what then? What would I have done on all those Sunday afternoons, without the band? I guess I could have been one of those sad blokes who does discos at other kids' parties, sitting slumped at the turntable all evening with everybody else dancing and no one coming up to speak to me. *You'll tinker with your electrical gadgets till the day you die.* That was Hugo's voice, and I wanted it out of my brain. But he was clever, Hugo, and not everything he said was wrong.

Besides, I was the man with the van. How else would the band get to Jed Alexander's festival? They needed me.

"OK," I said. There was a kind of jolt inside me as I said it, as if we'd climbed in the van, me and the rest of them, and I'd clunked the handbrake off – no, torn it off and chucked it out of the window – and slowly at first, then faster, we'd begun to roll downhill.

10

As soon as the light began to go, the road seemed too narrow, even though it was a motorway. There was a smeary sunset over Windsor Castle, all the colours of fire and smoke, as if the place was burning down again. After that I hardly noticed how the fields filled up with shadows and pulled in closer till there was only the night, like the walls of a one-way alley that gets darker as you go.

So we were on our way – to Cornwall, to Jed Alexander, to the festival. I rested my hands on the wheel and let the road take over. It was like a long, long slide. We'd climbed on a couple of weeks ago, when we said yes to Hugo's plan … or was it earlier, chanting on the precinct roof? Or earlier, in the phone booth, when we dialled Hugo's number? At the first gig? Or the evening we met Alia? The afternoon I told Ben, "You could be in a rock band"? No point in thinking those thoughts, Emod, I told myself. We're on our way. I could no more have pulled off at the next junction and pointed the van back to Borsley than I could have driven to the moon.

Over the chug of the engine I could hear their breathing settling down to sleep. Let them. I was better off without sleep. Too often lately it had brought those dreams. In the back of the van, packed in among the amps and gear, Clive and Alia had been quiet since Borsley. No small-talk there. On the bench seat beside me were Ben and Dee. They'd change places at the next stop, like musical chairs, but there were rules to this game, we all knew. Clive would stay in the back with his amp. We could have Alia and Dee in front, or Dee and Ben, but not the other permutation. Me, I was glad I was driving. I like to know where I am.

For a while Ben and Dee said small practical things. "Did you put in the can opener?" "There'll be one in the cottage. Hugo's fixed it all." Things like that. If you didn't look at them they could have been someone's mum and dad on the first leg of a family holiday. That was just what they'd be one day. Or so everyone thought, before Alia.

After a while they were quiet too, with Dee's head on Ben's shoulder. It was only the sound of the breathing behind me – slow and very deep, one of her meditation things – that told me Alia was awake. She'd be sitting very upright, very straight and still. What was going on in her mind? These days, I chose not to ask.

No one had argued much since Hugo started coming to rehearsals. Clive had sulked for a day or two, then come back, tail between his legs. "OK," he said, "if it gets us to the festival, I'll do it." Alia smiled. Once when she stopped us in mid-verse and said, "We don't need the band at all there – just a Japanese flute and a didgeridoo," Clive nearly went nuclear, but she didn't argue. Alia had changed again. There were none of her flights of fancy these days. She was quiet and organized and in control. Of course we'd keep Clive's bass line, she said. Afterwards she had a word with me about some electronic sounds I could weave in with the drum effects, and they came out suspiciously didge-like. Some of Ben's tunes got recycled, others quietly ditched, and of course there were Alia's songs.

We worked our hind legs off. Hugo never said a word, just sat there in the corner like a great carved effigy. When the rehearsal was over we'd have three or four new numbers under our belts. Then he would get to his feet, nod and walk out of the door. There was always a hush until we heard the *rhum-rrhumm* of his motorbike, then we'd start talking again the way we used to. Even Clive agreed, these days we got things done.

Hugo slipped me some samples of drum sounds and strange twangs and rattles. I recognized some from that tape of shaman singing, but some of the others were even weirder, with deep-down vibrations that make animals jumpy when there's going to be an earthquake. I played them on my head-phones in bed that evening, just to get used to them, and found myself lying there still dressed in the morning, with fragments of dream inside my head like broken glass. Where was I? In a lift-cage. All of us were in it, going down and down, getting darker and hotter till we reached this great cleft in the earth's crust. That's the Fault Line, Hugo whispered, and I saw a row of cages with their bars all buckled. I couldn't see the creatures but I heard them breathing. One more slippage, he said with a chuckle, and they'll all break free.

I didn't play the sounds again. I programmed them in with the drums where Alia wanted them, but I did it by the numbers on the visual display, and kept the sound down low.

TIREDNESS KILLS – TAKE A BREAK said the sign at the roadside, and I pulled off at a service station like a small lit island in nowhere. The others groaned and tumbled out into the car park, stiff and sore. In the Country Fayre café it was the night shift, with solitary drivers dotted round the tables, staring at yesterday morning's papers or at themselves in the plate glass windows. If you stared at your own face, close up, long enough it seemed to disappear. You could look right through it, like reflections on a pond when you suddenly realize that you can see the fish and tangled weed beneath. Then you saw the darkness and the curving trail of headlights and tail-lights snaking westwards, flowing like a stream of lava in the dark.

"Yes please?" said the waitress curtly. She'd taken one look at us – Ben's hair, Clive's tattoo – and put us down as trouble, you could tell. "All Day Breakfast," Clive grunted, "and a beer." Dee went for a salad, but she always pinched chips off Ben's plate. And Alia?

"Mineral water. Sparkling," she said.

"That all?" snapped the waitress. "Suit yourself." She marched off to shout down the hatch.

"I know you're on a diet," said Dee, "but that's ridiculous."

"It isn't a diet," said Alia. "It's a fast."

"You're cheap to run," said Clive. "We'll keep you."

Alia withered him with a look. "It purges the toxins," she went on to Dee. "Makes the mind clear. Samurai warriors used to do it before battle."

The food arrived, with a saucer of plastic relishes. "Here," said Ben, "at least have a chip."

Clive took a swig of his beer and belched.

"It's all right," said Alia. "I don't expect any of you to understand."

Night-driving. I like it. The white lines and cat's-eyes just pull you along. Plus we were going westwards, and it felt like downhill; after all, it looks like downhill on the map. Down the narrowing alley of Devon and Cornwall, to the place that was waiting for us. Hugo had it all fixed. And there was this tune, running through the night...

> *who am I*
> *you can't define me*
> *cage of bone*
> *you can't confine me*
> *if you dare to*
> *try and find me*
> *look in the eyes of the night...*

The Transit hummed and juddered, top speed sixty. Fifty miles of that, you're in a trance. All kinds of thoughts come floating up from nowhere. But I knew where this one came from. It was Alia's latest song.

> *father, mother*
> *you can't hold me*
> *did you think*
> *that you controlled me*
> *what's out there*
> *you never told me*
> *look in the eyes of the night*

"Look at that," said Alia quietly, beside me. It must have been past midnight, though the dashboard clock was on the blink. There had been no light but headlights and cat's-eyes for hours, but suddenly the moon was rising. Behind the black hulk of a hill, silver-grey clouds boiled up in its light like spray from a dangerous waterfall.

Dee was fast asleep beside Alia, her head against the window, cushioned on Ben's sweater. He and Clive were in the back, asleep, and when I hit a bump there would be grunts and snores.

"Look," said Alia. "It's so beautiful. Doesn't it make you ... shiver?" There was only her voice in the dark. "That hill, it's like an animal." She sounded younger, now I couldn't see her: like a little girl up way past her bedtime, half excited, half afraid. "You know, the way cats go when they're hunting, sort of long and low, when they're about to *pounce*." The last word was a small thrilled whisper. I thought of the cat in the car park, batting the terrified mouse to and fro, just for fun. What if we were the mouse now, driving right between the cat's paws? We were in a valley now. Low trees arched out of stone hedges, blotting out the moon. Suddenly she turned to me.

"I'm not going back," she said.

"What? Where?"

"Borsley. I'm not going back."

"Hold it, we told your mum..."

"Forget my mother."

"Hey, we promised her..."

Alia laughed, in a faraway way. "How can you *promise*? Anything could happen."

Screech. That was our brakes. Everything happened faster than I could take in, but my right foot knew what to do. It hit the brake. A black thing had dropped from the trees like out of nowhere, dropped and stopped and hung straight in front of the windscreen with its wings flared wide, blotting out everything. Yellow eyes as wide and gold as headlights fixed on me.

Look in the eyes of the night...

People who've been in crashes often say that there's a moment just before it happens: everything is in slow motion and you're very peaceful; you know there's nothing you can do to stop it and you know you're going to die but heck, why not?

Then the owl stroked the air with its wings and surfed up over our headlights and my foot hit the brake. A shudder of blue and white arrows leaped out of the sharp bend and the brakes bit, the tyres crunched on gravel and I nearly lost it in a skid. There was a jolt of dead-weights, bags and bodies shifting in the back. Someone swore in their sleep.

"Jeeez," I shuddered. "That was a near miss." We had come to a stop and stalled, six inches from the rusty railings. Straight behind them our headlights tipped the upper twigs of trees. There was a steep, deep drop.

"No," said Alia in a voice that could have been coming from miles and miles or years away. She was so calm it was frightening. "It knew what it was doing."

"*What?* It could have killed us."

She nodded. "And it didn't. It let us pass."

"Oh, come off it..." I said, faintly. There was a faint whiff of scorching. I glanced at the dashboard; the dials were flickering again. There's a short in there somewhere, said my practical mind, while something else said: that night in the Green Room, that night on the precinct roof ... burnt feathers, owl feathers... No. Don't think that.

Alia didn't reply. She was sitting there with a faint smile on her lips. She was cradling a bag in her arms like a child holds a pillow and I realized what it was. Hugo's drum, his ritual drum. He trusted her that much.

The drum with the owl. The Arctic owl, the bird of death that picks the shaman's bones clean so his spirit can fly free. There was an owl on the drum.

"Did you..." I couldn't help myself; I had to say it. "Did you do that?"

"What?" she said.

"You know what I mean. The owl. I know you ... *make things happen.* I've been watching you. I've seen."

"You haven't seen a thing," she said. "Not yet." I kept my eyes straight ahead, through the railings like a cage that held the darkness out, or us in. I could feel her looking at me. "You understand, Emod, don't you?"

"Leave me out of this. I'm just the..."

"...the man with the van? Oh, yeah?" There was a long pause.

"That time in the Green Room," I said. "I saw ... well, I saw something. Is that one of Hugo's tricks?"

"No! I worked it out for myself. I used to spend a lot of time looking in mirrors. I guess you know what that's like."

"Nope. I cracked all the mirrors in our house."

"Exactly," she said. "And if you'd been a girl? Think of looking in the mirror every day and hating what you saw there. *Hating* it!" She dropped her voice again. "All the boys mooning over ... you know who, who's thin and pretty, when you're fat and ugly..."

"Who? *You...?*"

"Shut up. You look in the mirror and that's what you see. You want to kill it, smash it, wipe it out. Then one night I found I could do it. If I concentrated hard enough – really wanted to do it – I could make my reflection disappear." She touched my arm. "Wouldn't you, if you could?"

I started the engine and moved off, gently so as not to wake the others. "Well?" she said after a while.

"Got to keep my mind on the road," I muttered. There was a flash of white light in the rear view mirror, as a single headlight leaped round the bend behind. It drew level with our rear bumper, revving, then spotted a slim chance as the next bend lurched towards us. The motorbike ripped past us, slaloming in as the bend lit up and an oncoming lorry loomed round, right out on the centre line. I blinked and felt the whack of air as the lorry slammed by, inches from us, but there was the motorbike's rear light, vanishing ahead. It couldn't be – there'd been no space – but it was. He had slipped through the gap – *the gap between life and death*, the words formed out of nowhere in my mind.

"What a nutter!"

"That was Hugo," Alia said.

"At least he'll be there before us," I said, "if he doesn't break his neck."

"Oh, yes, he'll want to get everything ready," she said, and there was something in the way she said it that made it clear she didn't mean making the beds or putting ten pence in the meter.

Horan's Place, he said it was, this cottage he'd fixed through a friend of a friend. No village name or anything. He'd hand-drawn us a map, the kind that works as long as you stick with the directions but the moment you lose them you're lost for good. Apart from the map, it could be anywhere or nowhere. All I knew was when we got there Hugo would be waiting for us, already in control. He'd be standing in the door with his big hand on the latch and the key in his pocket, raddled face expressionless as ever, masking all the things he knew and we didn't, all the plans he had in mind.

11

We didn't talk much for a long time after that. The road became smaller and darker and the bends were coming thick and fast. Alia was very still. All I heard out of her was inside my head. It was the last verse of her song:

> you can't touch me
> you can't reach me
> whispers soft
> as snow beseech me
> fingers cold
> as frostbite teach me
> look in the eyes of the night...

Then we crested a rise and the moon slipped the clouds off its back like Alia sloughed the black cape off on stage that other night. And as pale as her arms had been then, I saw the white and slender figures on the hill, huge, a dozen or more of them ranged out in a line as if they'd been waiting. A welcoming party. "Stop the van," said Alia urgently. For a moment I thought she was going to be sick or something, but her eyes were wide with wonder. "I've been here before," she whispered, face pressed to the windscreen. "In a dream."

As we jolted into the lay-by, Dee stirred. "What've we stopped for? Are we there?"

"Come on, all of you…" Alia reached across Dee for the doorhandle, and they both slid out together. "Hey!" said Dee. "It's cold out here…" She stopped. "What are they?" Ben was on his feet behind her. "Hey, Clive," he said. "Get your backside out here. This is weird."

There was a field, with a high wire fence around it and a red sign on the gate. Inside, along the hilltop, eerie in the moonlight, thin white columns rose. The air around us trembled with a whining hum. The sound of power. At the top of each column, maybe twenty metres up, three slim curved blades were turning, *swish, swish, swish*, like a sword being slipped from its scabbard again and again.

"What the hell is it?" Clive's face peered from the van door. "I was asleep."

"It's a wind farm," I said, "you know, renewable energy and all that."

"*Windmills!*" Clive said. "That's all we need."

Alia was staring through the fence. "Yes," she said quietly, without turning round. "It was a flying dream. The place was just like this, except ... yes, that's it, they were skeletons, skeletons of giants. Giant acrobats. A circus..." I tried to stop myself seeing what she said, but for a second the wind-vanes were maniacal non-stop tumblers, bodies bleached by the moonlight, dead but won't lie down. She gave a strange smile. "They were juggling with their bones."

"Hey, what's this girl *on*?" Clive groaned and crawled back out of sight. Ben was gazing through the wire. "Like beansprouts," he said, and I giggled, thinking of the café. Whatever Alia had, it was infectious. I know about turbines, of course. I could have told them how to wire one up, but who wanted a lecture? As the three-quarter moon sliced through the space between clouds I looked again and saw pale roots and stalks of grass that'd grown under a stone.

"Scythes," said Alia, "cutting the wind."

"Save that for a song," Dee was shivering. "Clive's right. Let's get back in the van." But Alia had other ideas. She gave the gate a rattle. Padlocked. DANGER, the red sign said. NO ENTRY EXCEPT AUTHORIZED PERSONNEL. Next moment she was climbing it, over the top in a neat vault, on her feet and running with her floppy black sweater flapping round her like a pair of wings.

"Hey..." Ben called. "It says danger!" Alia heard; she turned and laughed. Ben glanced at me, at Dee, at Alia, then he was swarming the gate. "Hey, don't

102

be stupid," I said, but he wasn't listening. That's why I had to go over too.

I dropped down and stumbled, then picked myself up. At once I felt it, stronger now: the hum of power in the air. Alia was running, skipping almost, in the moonlight, her hair flouncing up and whirling as she turned. The windmills seemed to grow as she came towards them, with her arms held up like a small girl asking her daddy to bend down, sweep her up and whirl her in a dance.

"Look out," I shouted. "It said Danger. Don't touch anything."

Ben caught up with her just beneath the closest windmill, and I wasn't far behind. Close up, it wasn't the perfect marble column it looked at a distance. You could see the metal casing, with bolts and rivets, and small rusty patches and a place where it sprouted a thick braid of wires. Alia turned, with her back to the windmill as if it was hers, and her skin glowed as white as its metal in the moonlight, as she threw her head back, looked straight up and laughed. The blades were right over our heads and their tips were a blur but I could hear the *whack* of each one as it passed. "Look," she said, "the moon!" From the angle we were standing, the swipe of the blades chopped out the exact bite-sized quarter that was missing from the moon. We were laughing together, too hard, like you do when you're scared and if you stopped you'd have to shout or cry.

Ben got his breath back first. "Let's get back to

the van," he said. "We're not meant to be in here."

"Who's going to stop us?" Alia said. "Who'd dare?" Her eyes were as wide as a hunting cat's, and glittering. "You can feel it too," she said, "can't you? We're getting closer to it all the time. This isn't Borsley now. It's everywhere down here."

"Sorry? What is?" I said.

"You know," she said to me. I shook my head. She grinned up at the windmill. "You know what I mean, don't you?" she said to it. "You know what it's like to have the *power*." She laughed and threw out her arms to embrace the moon-white metal and she gave a little yelp as she touched it as if it was cold.

"Don't you recognize the sound?" She closed her eyes. "Listen. They're chanting." And though it was crazy, I couldn't deny it was true. The beat of the blades was the thud of the drum, and I could see the bone-cartoons of owls and corpses trembling as a big hand, Hugo's big hand, stroked them. There was a nasal overtone of whirring bearings in the turbines, and through the stalk of the windmill came a creaking, throbbing deep in the throat like Hugo's shaman song. Alia took a deep breath and let out a long high note, like she had at Hugo's class that night, but twice as strong and twice as wild.

"Wings…" she murmured. "White wings…" Then she fell back, limp, unconscious, just like that.

"Can't you do something, Dee?" Ben's voice came from the back of the van. "Make her come round."

"She's fainted," Dee said. "That's all."

"Something's wrong with her, I know it. We should do something." Me, I kept driving. Alia still hadn't stirred. It hadn't been easy manhandling her back over that gate, not even with Clive and Dee helping, but it wasn't as hard as you'd think, because she felt so light. For someone that height she seemed to weigh nothing at all, as though she was really somewhere else and this was just the husk she left behind.

"The thing that makes me feel really bad," said Ben, "is her parents. I mean, they trusted us. We said we'd take care of her."

"Her?" said Clive. "Come on. It's not like she's a child."

"She's under sixteen," Dee said. "We *have* got to take care of her. Typical!" I kept on driving. The others could argue about her all they liked; I just wanted to get us to the cottage. Indoors, in proper electric light, we could be sensible. If Ben would just keep his mind on Hugo's map now it shouldn't be far.

She hadn't been electrocuted, that was something. At first Ben had shouted out, "Don't touch her," but I could see she wasn't twitching or in contact with anything.

"She's just exhausted," Dee said. "Been winding herself up, like she does. That fasting business doesn't help."

"What are we supposed to do?" said Clive. "Spoon-feed her? If she doesn't want to sleep or eat..."

"Yeah, and what if she passes out on stage?" said

Ben. "In front of Jed Alexander. Our big chance. Think of that. We've got to make her."

Dee snorted. "You ever tried to *make* Alia do anything? Save your breath."

We were on back roads now, so narrow that grass was growing down the middle. There were cork-screw corners and rocks jutting out on either side. "Are you sure this is right?" I said. Ben was holding the map to the inside light, which was flickering, and the dashboard clock had stopped just past midnight, which must have been an hour ago. All we had was this map of Hugo's, and all we could do was trust it. Other than that, well, who knew where we were, in time or place?

"This would never have happened if you hadn't stopped at the stupid wind farm." Ben was fraying, I could hear.

"*But Alia told me to…*" Dee mimicked. "Every-one gives in to her. Look at us now: she isn't even conscious and we're still at her beck and call."

The road had dropped into a wooded valley, with low crookbacked trees leaning over the rough boulder walls. At the bottom we bucked over a hump bridge, and a footpath sign flashed up a moment: *Horan's Leap.* Alia jolted and sighed. "Give her some air," said Ben, and I wound down the window. In came a soft relentless ripping sound: a river.

"We're almost there." Alia's eyes flickered open. "I can feel it."

"You OK?" said Ben anxiously. "You had us worried there."

"You passed out," said Dee. "You were dead to the world."

"No, I wasn't," said Alia in her quiet floaty voice. "I heard everything you said." Dee blushed. "It's OK," said Alia. "I was just ... outside..."

"Just get some rest," Ben said quickly. "Things always feel weird when you come round from a faint."

"I've never got so far before," said Alia in a hushed voice. "I was right outside my body, looking down..."

"For God's sake!" Clive snapped. "I can't take this stuff, not now, OK? It does my head in."

"You don't have to be afraid," said Alia quietly.

"Make her shut up," Clive said to Dee.

"There!" Ben pointed suddenly, and I swung between the rough-hewn gateposts, clipping the bumper slightly with a grating sound. "On down the lane," Ben said as we jerked and rattled between overgrown hedges that cracked whips of bramble in the headlights and scratched at the windows. Then we were going downhill again, lurching sometimes as the wheels slipped and I stamped the brakes on, till we jolted round a corner and came face to face with the woods. In our lights, they looked not green but grey.

On our right was a pile of shadow, where a rocky outcrop jutted out. Under the overhang, nestled up against it almost, was the cottage. The track stopped dead beyond it. Horan's Place it had to be.

"I thought he said *cottage*," Dee said. I could see her point. I'd rather imagined there'd be a thatched roof and that sort of thing. Whoever Horan was, he must have been small. But quaint it was not. The place was grey stone, eaves of grey slates coming almost down to head height, and tiny windows tucked beneath them, dark and blind. The only feature was a narrow porch, two single slate slabs and another on the top, that made a kind of coffin of the door. Out of the coffin stepped a figure, crouched at first, with his hand on the latch, because of the low door. As he stepped into our headlights two separate shadows of him, twice life-size, stood up behind him on the wall.

"Hugo," Ben said. "Alia's not well. She passed out."

Hugo's large face loomed in at the window, not looking at the rest of us at all. Alia lifted her head. "This is it, isn't it?" she said. "I can feel it." He nodded.

"Come on," said Ben. "We'd better get her to bed."

She pulled herself upright. "I'll be fine now," she said. "Just fine. The rest of you get some sleep. I'll join you in a while."

Inside, we climbed the steep stairs: Clive and Ben and Dee and me. Hugo and Alia watched us. We went meekly, like in any family any night of the week. We were children being sent to bed, while the grown-ups had their time alone downstairs.

12

There was a wildlife film I saw once: David Attenborough standing in a cave mouth as about a zillion bats streamed out around him, blackening the evening with their wings. In my dream there was a jolt and the Fault Line had shifted; the cages burst open and the things that had been down there in the darkness under lock and key started scrabbling and screeching in bat voices, bird-shrilling, rodent-squealing. Then they started to pour out as it dawned on them that they were free.

I'd been awake for about a minute when the feeling came to me: I had to get out of that house. Don't get me wrong. I'm not the type to get spooked by atmospheres. I know how they do it in films, with camera angles and background music. True, the place was cramped and dark, with crazy-angled ceilings and pink floral paper on the walls gone brown and crisped as if there'd been a fire. True, the one small window in each room faced straight out into trees or the rock behind the cottage; all of them seemed to let in more shadow than light. And I knew that my dream was just a dream. It wasn't that. It was my friends I had to get away from.

Even allowing for a bad night's sleep, they were being foul. We'd crashed out on the bedroom floor in our blankets and bedrolls, and no one had stirred till past dawn. Clive was the first to sit up.

"Hey, you guys, wake up," he said.

"Keep the noise down," Dee snapped. Half awake, she sounded strangely like her mother.

"We're playing a gig," said Clive. "THE gig. We've got to start practising *now*. Where's Ben?"

At first I couldn't see Ben either. Dee had bundled him into the corner, with herself between the rest of us and him. "Leave him alone," she said. "He needs his sleep."

"Bloody students…" Clive's voice was rising.

"Just shut up, OK?" Dee yelled. The sweetest, mildest girl I've met, and she was shrieking. "Look, now you've woken Emod."

I didn't look up. I rolled out of my bag and shuffled to the door. "Got to get some air," I mumbled, and creaked down the stairs. On the hearth mat Alia lay curled up like a cat, with a grey blanket over her and her hair splayed out, completely covering her face. She'd had some sleep, then. That was something. Where was Hugo? He was nowhere to be seen.

Outside the porch, the air was cool and close. So this was it, then, we were here? I looked back into the darkness of the coffin-door. Somewhere far in the past we'd wanted something, or Ben had, at least. Yes, to get out of Borsley, that was it. Something to do with freedom. And every step we'd gone had taken us somewhere smaller – the Arcana café, the shack on the mall roof, all of us crammed in the back of the van, and now this. You bet I wanted air.

The van was damp with the dew, as if it had been sweating in its sleep. The woods looked a greenish grey in daylight, with sparse leaves and a tangle of boulders and trunks and moss and creepers so you couldn't tell what was wood and what was stone. The track wound uphill, with our tyre-ruts in it, and I noticed Hugo's black bike leaned against the side wall, almost out of sight.

It was still. No sound, no birdsong, nothing. It was the kind of stillness that lays a cool hand on your shoulder, like outside the Green Room, all that time ago. I looked back at the cottage, but nothing had changed, then I looked up, and there he was. The overhanging shale still kept the house in shadow, and probably would all day, but perched on the lip of it sat Hugo in a rigid cross-legged pose.

If he had his eyes open at all, it was only a slit and he was motionless, more like a stone-carved Buddha

111

than a man. I waved out of habit, feebly; I forced him a grin but there was no reaction. So I turned to walk away, and then he spoke.

"Emod, my friend," he said. I looked up, squinting at the light. If it had been anyone else there would have been a slight sneer on their lips but there was nothing, no expression there at all.

"They're awake," I said. "I guess you'd better get them organized, if you're manager…"

He slipped sideways out of sight, and was down on the path beside me quicker than seemed possible. He stepped up close, too close for comfort, looming, then he smiled. "What do you mean," he said, "*if*?" For the first time I noticed, really noticed, the size of his hands, big square bone-crusher fingers, blunt nails on the end.

"I mean … I mean I think they need some things explaining. Like: where is this festival? And when do we get to meet Jed Alexander? And…"

"All in good time. We need to gather our strength." He let his hand rest on my shoulder and I thought of cars in wreckers' yards, the rattle of the steel chain as the big claw lowers down to grab them. "Make yourself at home," he said. "This is a very special place. A place of *power*. You'll see." As he turned away I noticed I was trembling, though I didn't know, or didn't want to know, why.

The path into the woods was slippy at first, down a steep bank, in and out of boulders, sometimes with mud underfoot, sometimes uneven stones half hidden by moss. The day was still heavy and moist, as though there might be thunder. A bird piped up and shrilled the same dull call-sign again and again, but after the hush round the cottage it felt like a sign of life. There might even be some wildlife in these woods. I stopped and listened. Had that been a movement in the bushes ... there?

There was a crunch in the undergrowth nearby. The hanging ivy quivered like a curtain and I waited for it to part, but whatever it was had stopped a moment; I could hear it panting, with a slight wheeze in its breath. Then it came on, and I slipped behind a boulder just in time to see it emerge.

The old woman's head was down, watching her feet, so at first all I saw was a tangled knot of grey hair where her face should be. She was picking her way through the undergrowth slowly, muttering, stopping to pant and grumble to herself, then moving on again. As she passed me I saw that her legs were swollen, purplish and painful to look at where they showed between the old tweed dress and the surgical bandages that covered them below the knee.

She took the bank in several stages, stopping every few steps, but at each stop she looked around her, looked and listened. At the edge of the woods she should have stepped out on to the track with a sigh of relief, but she didn't. She moved behind a tree and looked and listened. Just like me.

We were both still for several minutes. In the hush I could hear muffled voices in the house. Then they were clearer as the door opened, and people were going in and out, unloading the gear from the van, getting set up. There was the first blurt of an amp. There was going to be a practice. Fine. Now I'd wired up their beat box they could manage without me.

As for the old woman, she could have been simply resting on her stone, except for the way she craned forwards – watching, listening. As soon as the music began, she climbed the last few feet, then she hobbled across the mud track quickly and round to the side. *She knows where she's going*, I thought as she slipped past Hugo's motorbike – I had a crazy vision of her stealing it – and vanished round behind the house. There wasn't a back door, I knew. And she didn't look like a neighbour coming round to borrow sugar or complain about the noise.

I hardly needed to move quietly: the thud of the practice shuddered through the walls. "Hello?" I called, but she wouldn't have heard me. I crept round into the dark cleft behind the house. It was hardly an arm-span wide, almost roofed by the overhang, and there wasn't a way through; the cleft was blocked by a kind of lean-to made of single slabs of slate, like the porch. I could see her squat hunched back bent over as she tried the shed door. Tried and failed.

"Hello?" I said, louder. She turned with a jerk,

and her mouth dropped open. She was cornered, but she stood her ground.

"Now, you just let me pass, young man," she said. "No law against looking." Her face was round and bloodshot. Behind round glasses there were slightly skew-whiff eyes. There was a smell around her, sweat-and-earthy. In Borsley she'd have been a bag-lady, just a sad old thing.

"Sorry..." I said. "We're staying in the cottage. That's my friends in there."

"Ah..." she nodded. "You're a friend of *his*, then?"

"His?"

"The big man."

"Hugo? No, not a friend. We just know him."

"Hugo! Well, so that's what he calls himself, where you come from..." There was a knowing twinkle – I couldn't tell if it was malice or laughter – in those slightly crazy eyes.

"We're just here for the festival," I said. "That's all."

She cocked her head like birds do, angling for a worm. "That's all, is it?" she said, doubtfully. "I suppose you think this is one of them holiday lets."

"Isn't it?"

"What, Horan's Place!" Her face creased and she hooted silently. Then in a flash she was serious again. "Not exactly your dream cottage, is it?"

There was a hush inside, mid-verse, mid-song. That would be Alia, making problems. But the woman stiffened. "I'll be going now."

I went to move aside, then changed my mind. "Just one thing…"

"Let me pass." She tensed, and something flickered in her eyes, behind the glasses, that made me shiver and the gooseflesh stand up on my arms.

"I'm not stopping you," I said, stepping backwards. "It's just… You know Hugo?"

"I know enough. Stays here sometimes. No one else would, Lord knows. Even the Londoners – beg pardon if you're one – even the Brummies, God help us, they can feel it in the air."

"Feel what?"

"Oh, come on, this is *Horan's* Place…"

"Who is this Horan? Just tell me, then you can go."

"Who is he? Was. Mad old beggar, sort of hermit. Long time ago. Rest of the parish gave the place a wide berth, on account of his powers." She took a step closer. "Some of us knows how they felt."

"Powers?" I said. "What powers?"

She shrugged. "They called it old wives' tales, afterwards. But old wives know better than most. There's powers in this place, all right. Some of us knows that, and tries to see the powers get used right. Even if we do get called names for our trouble. Still, you don't get the ducking-stool these days, that's a mercy. Just a visit from the social worker." She grinned. "Horan? He could do bits and pieces, healing at first but he branched out when the village folk turned nasty. Still, it didn't save him in the end. Couldn't do it when he needed."

"Do what?"

She chortled. "He thought he could fly."

The band struck up again, slower, louder. It was *Look in the Eyes of the Night*. "Good to meet you," she said, squeezing past. That old unwashed smell, like earth and sweat, pushed me aside. "Now if you don't mind…"

"One more thing…" I said as she reached the corner. "What were you doing?"

"Doing? Nothing. Just keeping an eye on the place. Somebody's got to." She stepped back towards me and held out her hand. It felt small but pudgy, and rough around the nails. "Family business, really. Horan was my great-great-grandad. Mary Field," she said. "You see anything you don't like, anything at all, you ask your Auntie Mary. Anyone'll tell you where to find me…" Suddenly she was a bag lady, muttering old grudges to herself, again. "They're always watching me. Whispering about me when they think I can't hear." She gave a snort to herself and turned her back on me.

"Wait," I called after her. "What's in the shed?"

She squinted back, then shook her head. "You've had your *one more thing*," she said. "Don't ask. Just let it be."

13

ten thousand years I've been alone
the tick of the clock in a cage of bone
I thought it was locked, I never knew
I could step out of me, of me and you
stop the clock and step right through
into Real Time

I'd felt the beat from outside, like a big heart beating. I didn't recognize it. There were twangs and drones and echoes in it, too slow to be catchy, something creepier. I slipped in at the door and no one looked up, as though they were hypnotized, all of them together. It was one of Alia's new songs.

At the end of the verse she swung to look at Ben, and his fingers went scuttling up the fretboard, but his eyes were on her. It wasn't a show-off solo like he did at the club, more a series of bird cries or wolf howls, an echoey raw sound I'd never heard his cheap amp get before. Dee was hunched by the door, just staring. At the end of the solo, Ben glanced up and caught her eye, and the wolf howls faltered, fading back into common-or-garden feedback.

no one can follow, no one to blame
out of body, face and name
white bones picked by carrion crow
white owl flying, swirling snow
free as the cold wind, free to go
into Real Time

There was a crackling on Alia's mike, getting worse as the verse went on. It would cut out for a word or two, then cough back in. Loose connection – I'd fix it in a moment. But on the long soaring swoop of *into Real Time* it gave out and her voice was struggling through the music, faint and shrill. She threw the mike aside. "Nothing's working!" she said, as they came shambling to a halt and the drum sound thumped on, mechanical, alone. I threw its switch and it stopped in mid-beat. "We're losing it," Alia blazed coldly. "Something's getting in the way."

"We're tired, that's all," Ben said. "Let's take a break."

I squatted down behind the amps and got busy. Ben was just drifting after the others, to the kitchen or outside, when Hugo's voice came from the corner. "Well?" He'd been so still I hadn't seen him.

"What do you think of her now?" he said quietly – to Ben, not me. People forget I'm there, it often happens. "You feel the *power*?"

Ben grinned, sheepish. "You've said it. She's got power, OK."

Hugo shook his head. "You haven't seen anything yet," he said. "She's scarcely begun to tap it. We must simply ensure that nothing – and nobody – gets in the way." He let the words hang in the air a moment. "That last song…" he went on. "For a moment, your playing too had that certain something. Then…?"

Ben frowned. "I've been with Dee a long time," he said at last. "I'm very fond of her, I really am…"

"But?"

"But … but I was going for it back there, it was working … till she caught my eye. And then it was gone." Ben dropped his voice very low. "I like them both," he said, "in different ways. Dee keeps saying I must *choose*."

"The man with power," Hugo said simply, "does not have to choose. What he wants, he gets."

If Ben was going to answer he didn't have a chance, because Alia swept back in with the others behind her. "Can't see what's the matter," I said. "It looks OK." Ben had moved away from Hugo quickly, guiltily. "Let me have a look," he said.

"Alia broke it," Dee said under her voice. Alia had thrown herself down in the corner, with her knees up in front of her, peering between them. As

Ben bent down beside me, I whispered, "I heard what you said."

"I don't expect you to understand," Ben said under his breath. Where had I heard that line before? I bit my lip.

"I might not know much about it," I muttered, "but I know that two-timing only leads to grief."

"Oh, come on…" Ben gave a weary sigh. "Two-timing! *If I can keep two women happy what's the sweat?*" He was whispering, but the words came over loud and clear. They boomed out. Everyone was staring at us. I tapped the mike. *Puck, puck*, it went. The thing was on. Ben's face went white. He stared at me as though he thought I'd made it happen, then he looked at Dee.

She didn't shout, not straight away. For a moment she hung there quivering, as if there was something inside her just too big to come out all at once. "Go on," she said, in a choked voice, "broadcast it, why don't you? Make a public announcement. Tell them from the stage tonight, I don't care." In the doorway, she turned. "I don't care, because I won't be there to hear." The door slammed.

"Damn," said Ben, under his breath. "Damn, damn." Then he rounded on me. "You told me the bloody thing wasn't working."

I tapped the mike again. Dead. "That's because it wasn't," I said. "Look…" At the other end of the lead I was holding, the jack plug lay, a metre or so from its socket, unplugged on the floor. In the corner, almost hidden in the shadow, Alia watched us from between her knees. I couldn't see her mouth but I knew from her eyes that she was smiling, with that quiet knowing smile.

Ben stared at the plug. He shook his head. When things get too crazy, ignore them, that's the sanest thing to do. I was doing my best, but there were just too many of them. "I'd better go after her," said Ben, without moving. "I'll come with you," I said. When we got to the porch, I grabbed his arm and pinned him back against the slate. I closed the door behind us. Now we were private, in the coffin porch, as private as the grave.

"She did it," I whispered. "Alia did it."

"What?" He looked blank.

"The mike. I don't know how. There must be some physical explanation. But it was her, all right."

"You're cracked," Ben said.

"We're all cracked. Everyone's been crazy since we got here. It's this place…" But Ben was shaking his head again, in that *I-can't-handle-this* way. "Dee. Got to find her," he said vaguely.

She was sitting on the bumper of the Transit. There were dribbles of mascara down her cheek. "Emod," she said when she saw us. "Come and talk to me."

Ben lurched towards her. "Listen," he said, "I'll explain…" As he reached out his hand she flinched. He touched her arm. She slapped him, hard.

"Don't you lay your filthy hands on me!" She jumped to her feet. This was Dee. Nice, pretty, pleasant Dee. Her eyes were red and narrowed. "Get out of my sight." Ben's face went crimson, and I saw his fist clench. Quickly, I stepped between them.

"Thank you," Dee said sweetly. "Take a walk, Ben. I want to talk to Emod. He's the only one here who listens to me." And she looked me in the eye and smiled.

Now when blokes talk about the reasons why they fancy Dee – and believe me, nine out of ten of them do – they mention lots of things, her long brown hair, her model-shape midriff, the cute way the end of her nose wrinkles when she talks, but they always come back to her eyes. Dee's eyes are big and brown and sort of pleading. Now they were all smudged and puffy but still, I could see how you might want to put an arm around her. Just to make her feel all right.

Behind me, Ben let fly one foul swearword, spun round and made for the door. Dee touched my arm gently, but at the same time I saw her eyes flicker sideways, to make sure Ben had noticed...

"Leave me out of this," I said. "Go and sort it out with Ben, for Christ's sake." Those gentle brown eyes of hers narrowed again, and blazed.

"You're useless," she said. "Can't you do anything right?" And she turned away. I stood there for a minute, feeling useless. She was right. "Just leave me alone," she said over her shoulder. I looked at the door of the cottage, dark and small. The last thing I wanted to do was go back in there. I'd have climbed in the van but Dee was sitting on it, sulking fiercely. My van. I made for the edge of the woods, where the path led down, just for somewhere to go.

The bank was scuffed where I'd been down it earlier. A couple of steps down, I glanced back in case someone was watching, but they weren't. As I turned my foot snagged on a bramble and I pitched forward as if someone had caught hold and yanked. When I opened my eyes I was lying wedged against a boulder. Close up, I could see a woodlouse like a prehistoric try-out for a tank, rumbling towards a barbed-wire entanglement of prickly lichen. High above it, coming into focus gradually, was Mary Field.

"Running away?" she said. "You want to tell me about it?"

I shook my head. It ached. "Better get back." I levered myself upright, swayed a moment, then my knees gave way. I flopped down on the boulder.

"You're right," she said. "You and your friends aren't cracked. It *is* the place."

"You were listening!"

"Just keeping an eye out," she said. "Like we Fields have always done, since my great-grand-mother's time."

"You mean, you look after the place? You're the caretaker?"

Mary Field smiled. "You could say that, yes. Taking care. You take care too," she said, and the smile vanished. "If he takes you out the back, don't let him lock the door."

14

When I got back inside the cottage it was quiet. No hum of amps, no sounds of practice. There was Clive's voice, sounding edgy, then Hugo's, very soothing, from the sitting room.

"You haven't told us anything," Clive said. "We don't even know what time we're on."

"10.30, this evening."

"And nobody's been to see us. Nothing about contracts, or the sound, or lights…"

"That's all being taken care of." It was Hugo's lion-purring voice. "That's why you need a manager, to take care of these things for you."

"…And we haven't *seen* the place yet. We should give it the once-over. Hear some other bands. We can't just walk out there and play."

"We need to gather our strength," said Hugo. "Why do you think I've brought you here? Yes, you could mix with the crowd..." You could hear the slight curl of his lips as he said it, slowly. "You could hear some bands, get a bit drunk ... just like all the others. Is that what you want? Is that what *we* want?"

I was in the doorway by now. No one glanced up, as usual, though I was smeared with mud and probably had lichen in my hair. Ben and Alia were looking at Clive in just the way Hugo intended. Clive looked at the floor, and didn't reply. "We are wasting our power," Hugo went on, "with these squabbles. Trust me. Let me show you something. Then you'll understand why this is such a special – such a powerful – place."

"Count me out," said Clive. "I'll play the songs, OK? I'll do double-back somersaults if it means Jed Alexander gets to hear us. But when it comes to the mystical stuff, count me out."

For a moment Hugo loomed above him, and I thought: *first Geek goes, then Dee. Is it Clive's turn? And who's after that?* Then without warning Hugo smiled. "Fine," he said lightly. "You're tired. Take things easy. There's beer in the kitchen. Grab some sleep. We'll just be outside at the back." I don't know if I gave a little gasp then, or if he'd had one eye on me all the time. "Emod..." he said. "Come and join us. I think you'll find it interesting..."

I could have said no, of course. But what would be the point? If I'd meant no, I'd have said it weeks ago. We were nearing the end of the long slide, sliding faster; it was getting steeper. Why else had we come all this way, if not for this?

There was an iron fob-watch padlock on the lean-to door. Hugo had the key. It seemed natural that Alia went first when he held the door open. Ben followed, then me, and as we blinked at the dark Hugo bulked in after us and pulled the door behind him. There was a clunk: a bolt, my ears told me, not the padlock and key.

"What you are about to see," Hugo's voice came in the darkness, "very few people know about. It must stay that way." A match flared in his hands and Alia picked the iron candle holder off a shelf. As the flame took the wick, light washed over her face, and I was in the Green Room, as I'd been so often in the dreams where the mask that was Alia's face pulled tight and ripped and peeled away. Those dreams were with us now, like the other dreams where I was in a cave, a fault, deep underground. Alia's face tonight was thinner and paler than I'd ever seen, with purplish shadows round the eyes that weren't make-up or tricks of the light. In my mind's eye the living skull face grinned its grin again, and Alia was halfway there.

As Hugo led the way, I brushed against the shed door. My hand found the cold edge of an iron bolt and slid it, very quietly. Then I followed the others, as their shadows flapped and billowed round the candle-light.

If the rock face had been all there was to the back wall, the lean-to would have been no bigger than a garden shed, and like all garden sheds, it was heaped up with old planks, fence posts, tools and jars and cans. But the floor sloped away and opened back into a corner overhung by overlapping shelves of shale. At the back, Hugo stepped straight into a shadow, the whole bulk of him, and vanished. Then Alia's candle lit the edges of a narrow cleft. It was a tight squeeze, even for me, but the rock was smoothed and blackened, as if worn away by water, or by many bodies. As Ben's filled it, blocking out the light, I held my breath and pushed through after him, as quick as I could go.

The air was cool in there, not like the thundery heat outside. The inner chamber wasn't large, but the candle-light seemed to thin out and dim. The walls had no outlines yet, random shadows and bulges of stone. There were small lights wriggling on the back wall, as glossy as worms, and gradually I made out the sheen of trickling water, where reflections of our candle slid and squirmed. Alia laid the candle in the middle of the floor, and we squatted in a circle round it. Hugo hadn't told us; it had seemed the only thing to do.

We were silent, glancing at each other's faces, then at Hugo's, lit up by the flame.

"Look at the walls," he said, and as our eyes became accustomed the bulges and shadows seemed to shuffle to a different order and I began to understand. At first it seemed like random cracks and squiggles, and maybe that's all I'd have seen if it weren't for the fact I'd seen the shapes before. Stick figures, striding, leaping, hunting. As the candle flame flickered they wriggled and danced. There was something with horns, rearing up, and there were figures fallen, limbs dismembered, and was that a bird, with staring headlight eyes, in flight, scratched in the stone?

"You see," said Hugo, "why this must be secret? If official busybodies found out there'd be so-called experts all over it. They'd make a museum of it, they'd pick it apart and catalogue it. They would close it to the only people who could really *understand*..."

He looked from Alia, to Ben, to me... "People have found *power* in this place for thousands of years, thousands even before the pagan Celts turned it into a shrine. They worshipped springs, as you know. The living water, and the severed head." A hush closed round us. I could hear the candle whispering.

"Hard for us to imagine," he went on in a low voice, "how they would have seen it, the initiates. There would have been a ritual. Terror. A sacrifice, certainly. And in the niches in the walls, the heads..."

"H-how do you know all this?" It was meant to sound calm, an intelligent question, but my voice came out wobbly, bouncing back off the ceiling like a worried crowd of ghosts. Hugo looked at me a moment, then reached behind him to a recess in the wall.

The object he held when he turned back, cupped in two hands like a drinking vessel, was a shallow bowl. He turned it at an angle so it filled with candle-light. It was greyish-greenish, with a biscuity texture, more like coral than clay, and a zigzaggy crack, very fine, ran right across; the curve was not round, more a domed shape... And then I realized. Held the other way up, it would be the crown of a skull.

"You do see, don't you," he said again, "why these things must be secret?" His voice was hardly louder than the candle flame. "All real power is secret. And if anyone betrayed it, we would have to punish him." He looked at me. "You do understand this?"

I swallowed, and nodded. He got to his feet and stood above us, so much like a priest that when he reached into his leathers and pulled something out, something that glinted dully, I thought it was a cross. It was a knife. Very slowly he started to pace around us. Behind Alia he paused. She did not turn or flinch or blink. Her face tightened, and the bones of her cheeks were outlined in shadow, as if the skin was drawn back as tightly as her hair. I could see little tucks at the corners of her mouth and eyes, as if she was fifty, not fifteen, and for a second it was my grandmother's face as I'd seen it for the last time, propped up in her hospital bed. I blinked and it was Alia again. Hugo moved on. Behind my back he paused, and my back hairs tingled.

Moments. Minutes. He moved on.

The knife flashed. Ben flinched, and Hugo stepped into the circle with a couple of inches off the end of Ben's precious ponytail. Bending down, he fed it to the candle; it crackled and flared and the cave was filled with its burnt stink. "Just a little sacrifice," he said, and smiled.

We did the chanting, much like in his eyrie on the precinct roof. Hugo began without warning, with a single rustling breath, more like sighing than singing. Alia's breath joined his, and Ben's, and maybe mine, I don't know, because there seemed to be others, dozens of them, hissing echoes coming out to join us from the walls.

Hugo stopped first. When we looked up, he had the skull-cup in his hands again. He dipped it into a pool where the trickle of water gathered from the back wall, then he held it out, level with our faces, like an offering. Ben took a sip, frowned at the taste, and passed it on. I tilted it quickly, trying not to let it touch my tongue. Alia laid it on her lips a moment, like a cold kiss, before drinking. Hugo laid the bowl beside the candle, solemnly. In the light, the little drop of water still in it was a cloudy red.

Iron oxide, I thought. Rust. That's why it tasted like that...

Hugo reached back into the pool and pulled out

something like a sodden towel. Sodden, dripping, darkly stained… He dropped it alongside the bowl and the candle, so its legs and tail flopped at squeamish angles, and Ben gagged and choked. It was a cat.

I'd seen Hugo smile before, even grin, but now he laughed out loud, and the echoes of his laughter boomed and echoed round us, fading slowly when he folded his lips round his stained uneven teeth and stopped.

"Disgust," he said, "is Mother Nature's last desperate effort to control you. Taboos. To keep you beasts of burden, creatures of the herd. Break her hold, and you can be like gods."

In the horrible silence, Alia reached out for the cup and drank again.

"Well, I never," said a quiet voice from the entrance. Mary Field. How she had squeezed her swollen body through that crevice I couldn't imagine, let alone doing it silently, but there she was. She stepped out of the shadow heavily, as if it hurt. "Never seen such a performance in all my born days," she chortled, mirthlessly.

Hugo was on his feet in one bound, glaring, but she didn't back away. She took a step towards him, peering closer as if to make *quite sure* in the flickering light.

"Let's have a look at you then," she said. "Playing at being the village magician again?" I didn't look. Even with my eyes closed I could feel the weight of

Hugo bearing down on the old woman like an iceberg on a paddle steamer. "Going to hit me, are you?" she crowed. "You, hit a frail old woman? You with your famous *powers*?" She cackled, just for a moment like the witch some people said she was. "Go on, show your little disciples what you really are. Their great guru ... a bully, a fraud."

His hands went out as if to hoist her by the shoulders – waist-height to him. Something flashed in her eyes, like a black spark, and Hugo's hands stopped as if clamped in mid-air.

"Well, then," said Mary Field quietly. "They used to say that old man Horan could curse people just with a look. There's *powers* for you. Come on, look me in the eyes." Their eyes met. No one moved, but the two of them hung in the candle-light like arm-wrestlers quivering at the point of balance, deadlocked for a moment before one arm or the other buckles and is slammed down. No one breathed for a minute, for two... Then Hugo winced like a slapped child, lost eye contact, looked away.

"Ach," said Mary Field. "There's nothing in you. All talk." She sounded almost disappointed. "I'll leave your young friends to think what they will." She had been braced, every ounce of her bulk poised like a weightlifter's for the big lift. Now she relaxed and turned back to the entrance, looking old again.

"You smelly hag!" Alia was on her feet, screeching. Hugo staggered aside, caught in the shock-wave. "Stupid and fat. You don't know what you're doing…"

"Don't I, then? And what does a slip of a thing like you…?" Mary Field half turned but she was caught off balance. She stopped in mid-breath. Alia was next to her now, glaring. Mary Field gave a gasp. "Oh, so it's *you*…" Her voice was fainter. "I knew somebody had it in them. I thought it would be him…"

"Get out," hissed Alia.

Mary Field was backed against the rock now, shaking her head. "Stop this," she said hoarsely. She couldn't look up; she'd spent the strength she had on Hugo, but this was the girl, the sickly slip of a girl she'd been trying to save. "Stop it," she whispered. "Stop before…"

"Before what?" sneered Alia, merciless.

"Before it eats you up."

Alia's eyes narrowed slightly, her lips parted and the sound that came from them was like nothing I'd heard, somewhere between the whish of a slingshot and a hawk's cry. Mary Field's big body jerked. She groaned as if something had hit her, but instead of crumpling like they do on films she became rigid. Then she went down like a felled tree, and began to shudder and her lips began to foam.

15

"I didn't touch her!"

Mary Field lay on the cave floor, jerking. Alia had shrunk back. She was shuddering too. Ben was down on his knees beside the old woman. "Look," he said, "blood." Trickling through the sparse grey hair it looked dark, but it came off bright red on his fingers. "She's hit her head. I don't like this."

Mary Field was shuddering, arms straight by her sides. Her neck had arched back till the tendons looked like cables under pressure, ready to snap. Her face was dead white and her breath came in shudders, with a breathy bubbling in it, horribly like Hugo's shaman chanting. "Quick!" said Alia, shrilly. "Ben, do something…"

"Don't touch her." That was me. When I was in primary school this kid in our class had a fit. He just keeled over during PE and started writhing as if the Invisible Man had jumped him and wrestled him to the ground. We'd all seen faints before but this was nothing like it, and some of the kids started crying and someone screamed, "Miss, is he dead?" When it was all over she sat us all down and told us it was only epilepsy, just an illness, but I could see she was scared too. Later I looked it up in the library. The encyclopaedia said something about "electrical activity in the patient's brain".

"She's cracked open her head," said Ben.

"Send for a doctor?"

"No!" It was the first time Hugo had spoken since the duel. As we watched, the old woman's convulsions stopped abruptly and she lay there like a beached whale, huge and limp. "Get her out of here," he said.

The cleft seemed even narrower than on our way in. Mary Field's body was a dead weight and we had to roll it on its side to squeeze it through. Ben was outside, pulling at her feet, with Alia fighting to grasp the bloated legs and keep the dress from riding up so that the huge hips jammed completely. Once or twice she retched; if she hadn't been fasting for – how many days now – she'd have been sick. Back in the dark, Hugo was forcing the shoulders. By feel, I tried to catch the head to stop it bumping on the stony floor. I couldn't see but I could feel the blood.

Halfway through, the head rolled to one side, and groaned. She squirmed but her body was wedged. I pulled back, jammed against Mary Field and Hugo in the tight space, as she struggled, whimpering like someone in a nightmare. Hugo braced his feet against her for a great shove, and Mary Field's head slipped from my hands and hit the floor. Then she was quiet again.

In the light at the back of the house she looked ghastly. "She could be dying," said Alia in a flat, shocked voice. The first thing Hugo did was lock the door. Only then did he look at the body. "Get her in the van," he said, nearly in command again. "Emod, take her ... somewhere."

"To the village," Ben said. "There'll be a doctor."

"And then? What do I say?"

"Say nothing," said Hugo. "Leave her and go." He turned to me. "If you say a word about ... here..." That was enough. As we loaded the back of the van I tried to think of the weight in our arms as a carpet, damp and mouldy from a cellar. Not an old, sick woman. Not that, no.

"I'll come with you." We'd forgotten about Dee. All this time she'd been sat in the front seat, sulking. Whatever speech she'd been planning for Ben, it vanished when she saw us. Her mouth came open in a soundless *What?* but nobody was volunteering any answers. Only as we pulled up the muddy track and out of sight, she turned to me.

"Emod, what's happening? Why won't they say?"

"Don't ask," I said. "Not now. Later."

"But *what*...?"

I slammed on the brakes. "How do I know?" I

guess I was shouting. "She just appeared. No one touched her. Epilepsy, won't that do?" Dee stared with big scared eyes. Her lip quivered but she didn't speak. "OK," I said, taking a deep breath. "Let's be calm. Just let me drive. We'll talk about it … when it's over, right?" In the back, Mary Field was making her waking-from-a-nightmare noise again. "Better get in the back with her," I said. "Just hold her hand."

"Excuse me," chirped the receptionist. "Have you an appointment?"

We'd got Mary Field on her feet, mumbling and teetering, and between us we steered her through the health centre door. Suddenly her legs buckled and we caught just enough of her weight to ease her down to sitting, propped against a rack of leaflets. Warnings about smoking in pregnancy, solvent abuse and healthy diets slithered round her as the whole waiting room shuffled out to stare. Dee had backed to the door, so everybody looked at me.

"We found her," I said. "Up the road. Just lying," I said. "Lying…" I trailed off. There was an uneasy silence. Then an old man with a zimmer snorted. "Ach," he said. "That Mary Field… Don't you pay her no mind, boy. Always being brung in like this. Queer old biddy."

"And the whole family of'n," put in the woman next to him. "Far back as anyone can remember, all that lot's been queer."

Mary Field shifted and groaned. The old man stepped back; the old woman crossed herself quickly. Then the doctor's door swung open. Before he could say, "What seems to be the matter?" I had grabbed Dee by the wrist and steered us out of the door.

Neither of us spoke till we were in the van and driving. At the end of the village high street, she said, "Stop!"

"What?"

"Just stop. Right..." She opened the door. "Thanks for the lift, Emod. I'll see you."

"Just a mo..."

"You heard what I said." She jumped out. "Whatever's going on," she said, "you're in it as deep as the rest of them. I'm off. I'm going home." She crossed the street quickly, then turned and called back. "I'm going to phone my mum and dad. And Alia's too." Then she cut down the side street, out of sight.

I stared after her. *Useless, Emod...* Her voice came back, but it could have been Ben's, or Hugo's, or Alia's. *Can't you do anything right?*

There was a bang on the driver's door. Somebody knocking. This is it, I thought. The police. They'll have come from the doctors. They'll say: *I have to caution you...* That woman will have died.

It wasn't the police. It was two girls, hitching. Everything about them – tie-dye T-shirts, headbands, patchwork bags – said *festival*. "Thought you were stopping for us," said one in a Birmingham accent. "Then we saw your friend get out, so we weren't sure." She glanced in the back. "Hey, you in a band?" she said. "You playing? Really?"

"Hop in," I said. "I'm going past the site. I'll drop you off."

"*Transformer…*" the other girl said as we drove off. "Doesn't ring a bell. Oops, sorry, shouldn't say that, should I?" She hauled a festival programme, folded into tatters, from her bag. "What time did you say? Nah, can't see anything about Transformer." She grinned. "You're having us on, aren't you? You're not really playing."

"Late booking," I said vaguely as I pulled up. People were still arriving. Battered cars and vans and convoy buses brought each other to a halt, with people walking in among them. There was a throb of music over behind the trees, and I could see the top of the scaffolding awning that must be the stage, and either side of it, even higher, two towers of speakers and lights.

"Let's have a look." I grabbed their programme and read through, and through again. "Another cock-up," I said. "Can't trust these agents…"

They gave me a sidelong look. "Ah well, thanks for the lift anyway."

There was a honk of horns behind me. In front, a policeman in an orange traffic-duty jacket was wagging his hand at me, flagging me on. I drove on.

It wasn't till I was most of the way back to the

cottage that I noticed: I was driving slower and slower. I kept stopping to let oncoming cars go past. I was finding excuses. Down by the bridge there was a lay-by where the sign said Horan's Leap, and I pulled over. I opened the window and let the sound of running water wash in, and I closed my eyes and sighed. I just didn't want to go back.

Not yet, at least. We've got to do this evening's gig, I thought. If there is one. But after that, no more. We would have to tell Hugo somehow: this has gone too far. In the morning, maybe. But this evening had to be the end.

In the crease of the seat beside me something caught my eye. In their hurry to get out they'd dropped something, those two Brummie girls. A book. *THE JED ALEXANDER STORY* said the cover. I picked it up idly – anything to put off facing Ben and Alia and Hugo – and began to read.

The shadows of the trees had shifted when I next looked up. It must be nearly evening. They'd be wondering what had happened. Good, I thought vaguely, let them worry. But I had other things to think about, just fragments and loose ends at first but as I shuffled them they were starting to join together like a jigsaw – not just 3-D but forwards and backwards in time too – in my mind.

Page 13. Jed Alexander forms Entropy, the name they'd use until he got big enough to be billed with his own name alone. In the 1967 photo he looks young and quite clean in his Afghan jacket, and most of the band are fresh-faced, with their long hair neatly combed. By the next photo, page 24, they're seriously scruffy. They're on the road, it's 1968 and there's a whole crew of roadies and groupies. The flower shirts have been replaced by darker things and leather. The ones without beards have got stubble and a gaunt look round the jaw.

Page 33: 1969, shortly before their new album went gold. Same crowd but smaller. Some of the back-up crew have vanished. So has one of the band. *The band's new line-up*, says the caption, *after the accident*. Accident? I flipped through the chapters. I didn't remember anything about an accident. 1969... Then I found the footnote, small-print as if they were trying to hide it, at the bottom of page 39.

None of the band have spoken publicly about the 1969 American tour. The death of an unnamed groupie went almost unreported in a year of famous rock deaths, though Rolling Stone *mentioned rumours of involvement in magical rituals, orgies and of course the party at which the dead girl leaped from an upstairs window, claiming she could fly. None of this was unusual in 1969. But "Klaus" Hughes left the band, or was fired, in circumstances no one has explained.*

I turned back to the photos. Apart from Jed himself, it was hard to tell which member of the band was which, they changed their styles so often. But I narrowed it down. The lean one at the back in

1968: imagine him without the beard. With hair not flopping round the face, but tied back with a leather thong.

Yes, scratch in the lines of age and hard living. Remember the man left the band when they were still struggling, just before the big break, and was not heard of again, so he'd be poor, and bitter. Set the gaunt pose, held here for the camera, as if in a mask, and hold it for thirty years.

I looked hard in the eyes of the photo as if it might suddenly own up and speak. As if it might say, "Good to meet you, Emod. Yes, you've guessed. 'Klaus' Hughes is Hugo. Me."

16

The cottage seemed empty when I got back. No one rushed to the door or windows. If they were watching out, I couldn't tell. There was the same dull stillness as there'd been all day, only heavier now, thundery. In the small patch of sky I could see from the valley, greyish haze was mixing with the evening blue. I pushed open the front door silently, from instinct. Everything was secretive round here.

The door to the kitchen was open, so I caught a glimpse of them before they saw me. Ben and Alia. Of course.

It wasn't a passionate clinch, far from it. Maybe that was what was shocking. He was at the sink, saying something, with his back to her. As I looked she stepped up close behind him and touched him gently on the nape of his neck, just below the lopped-off ponytail. As if she'd pressed a switch, he turned, and put his arms around her. For all I know, it was the first time, because he looked surprised, as if he couldn't quite believe the feel of her, then he squeezed, squeezed till her face was crushed against his shoulder. The words that popped into my mind were: *like a drowning man clutches a straw.*

Alia had never been your waif type, she was tall and big-boned, but now Ben's arms could have gone round her twice. Her soft edges had gone. Have you ever used a magnifying glass, on a piece of paper, to catch an image of the sun? You know how at first the spot of light is big and blurry but as you move the glass closer it shrinks and gets brighter and hotter till the paper smoulders? She'd been focusing inwards for weeks now, getting brighter, harder. The heat in the air, and those thundery clouds, were the smouldering. Any moment now something would burst into flame.

Ben looked up. "Emod!" He let go of her sharply. The only expression on Alia's face was the slightest secret smile.

"It's OK," I said, "I'm alone." His eyes flickered. "Dee's gone home," I said. There was a pause. I watched Alia's face for some reaction, but there was nothing. She'd learned to control herself that well. "That woman," she said. "Is she…?"

"Not dead," I said dully, "if that's what you mean. And no, I didn't say anything. No one knows anything about what happened to her."

"Is she conscious?" said Alia.

"She's not talking. And she's a local eccentric. No one will believe her when she does."

"That's OK, then," said Alia.

"Is it?" I looked at Ben. He looked at the floor. Then there was a footstep on the stair behind me, and there was Hugo. Straight behind him, as if being led on a string, came Clive.

"Hi, gang." Clive's eyes wouldn't quite focus. But then, I thought, he's been sleeping since morning. "Hugo's told me all about it," he said, groggily. "He's explained everything."

I took a deep breath. "I've seen the programme. We aren't in it. Not a word. 10.30? Nothing... Did he explain that?"

"Matter of fact," said Clive, "he did. There's a slot between bands, see, and this mate of Hugo's, he can slip us in. Like a surprise."

"You mean: Jed Alexander doesn't know?"

"Not yet," Clive grinned. "There's all these organization men, they control the business, run the record label, all that. He's like a prisoner of them, all the money men. We just gotta get past them, it's for his good. Because when he hears us..."

"He'll get us thrown off? Locked up?" I suggested.

"Far from it," said Hugo. "I know Jed Alexander. I know what he needs to hear. I know what will reach him, deep down in his soul. All it needs is a couple of songs. Believe me," he inclined his head to Alia, "you'll hit him right between the ears."

∗   ∗   ∗

"You didn't have to do that."

Ben, Clive and Hugo were outside, loading the gear in the van. For the first time all day, maybe, Alia was on her own, in the under-stair cupboard. "I mean Mary Field," I said, pulling the door to behind me. She was flashing a torch around, looking for string or something, but all at once it seemed to be very important. Anything rather than turn to face me and reply.

"You made it happen," I pressed on. Suddenly she swivelled. In the torchlight, shadows gave her black mascara. "You're to blame as much as me. Who let her in? It *was* you, wasn't it?"

"Why would I do that?" I hedged.

"Because you're afraid, of course. It's only natural. Afraid of the things that are starting to happen. Aren't you?" I looked away.

"Don't be!" she whispered and rested a hand, her weightless fingers, on my shoulder. It would have been easy, so easy, to turn like Ben did in the kitchen, turn and…

"You said *you* were afraid, remember?" I said. "After the last gig. *I'm afraid of what I might do…*"

"That's changed. I'm in control now." Her fingers tightened slightly. Through my sweater, I could feel her nails. "Please don't be afraid of me, Emod."

"Not afraid of you," I muttered, turning to face her. "I'm afraid *for* you, Alia." She laughed, with a strange tight grin that pulled back her cheeks as if they were worked by strings. I shuddered. The face in the mirror. One step closer.

"Alia, that time, in the Green Room…"

"I know. You said."

"I didn't say *what* I saw, did I?" For the first time, I saw her hesitate. She looked at me warily. She didn't know.

"There was nothing to see. Just a candle."

"The face," I said. She shook her head.

"It disappeared. I saw it."

"What if it was still there, somehow? If you can't get rid of things? If they come after you?"

Her eyes were very deep now, and her face was close to mine. "Stop it," she said. "Don't you know I'm happy? For the first time ever? You know what it's like, being the odd one – always feeling you've said the wrong thing, done the wrong thing, just *been* wrong." Her voice was trembling. "Well, she's not me any more, that stupid fat kid. Understand? She's dead and gone."

On the word *gone* she clamped her hand over the torch and the darkness closed round us, in our wooden box beneath the stairs. For a moment nothing seemed lit in there except Alia's hand. You know the thing small kids do when they're camping, telling scary stories round the fire. They put a torch against their palm and the light comes right through like an X-ray. You can see the bones. But that wasn't the worst thing.

Gradually my eyes made out the faint glow that her glowing hand cast on her face. She was watching it too, and her eyes glowed with excitement, not horror, at the shadows of her own bones and the thin layer of flesh that glowed orangey-red as if it was on fire.

"Alia? Emod? Let's get going." Ben's voice called from miles and miles away.

It'll eat you, Mary Field had said.

Alia looked up, waiting for me to say something, but I couldn't. I couldn't find the words, although – if I believed in that sort of thing – I might have said: *Yes, I'm frightened, Alia. Frightened for your soul.*

"Stop the van," said Alia suddenly. "I need some air."

"What is it?" Hugo revved in behind us, in the lay-by at the bridge. "It's Alia," Ben called back. "She's come over all strange."

She was out by the bridge now, sitting on the parapet. The air was close and hot, but she was shivering. Hugo slipped off his helmet and crouched down beside her, blocking the rest of us out. I thought I heard her whisper, "I can't. I'm afraid."

I'd seen Hugo thwarted before, I'd seen him angry and frustrated. *Now*, I thought, *he's going to blast her.* I was wrong. He reached up a hand to her face, rather gently, and lifted it towards him, shaking his head sadly all the time. "No," he said.

"It's them. The rest of the world. The ones who teased and bullied you, remember? Teachers, parents, so-called friends? They've always been frightened of you, because you're special. So they're trying to make you frightened too." He looked round at all of us. "Not only Alia," he said. "Emod? And Ben, you know the type I mean. Little people of Borsley, trying to make you just like them. Clive's bosses, giving him jobs a machine could do better."

"Yeah, and Jed Alexander's cronies…" It was Clive, with a fire in his eyes I'd never seen before. "The record labels and the agents and the gig promoters and the money men… Come on, Alia, let's screw 'em." She looked up and, weakly, smiled.

"It's always been the same," said Hugo. "You bet they whispered things about the men who did those carvings, and the shaman with his drum. And what they did to Horan…"

"What?" I said.

"Drove him out of his cottage. All the village folk, when they'd been whispering, when they were afraid. They called him a pagan, a sorcerer, a witch, a black magician … just because he had a little – just a little, mind you – power." The sound of the waterfall below seemed to swell up to meet him as he looked towards it. "They chased him into the valley, down to the edge of the fall. Why do you think they call it *Horan's Leap*? They pushed him to the edge and said: *Sorcerer, fly!*"

"And did he?" Ben said.

"The skull in the cave," said Hugo quietly, "is his."

Alia was on her feet again. "I want to see the place," she said.

Under the bridge, as the road cut steeply upwards on either side, the river cut suddenly down. The path dropped with it and we followed, slipping on mud or muddy stones but hardly feeling when we fell. The stream was beside us one moment, frothing in the moonlight, then it swerved between boulders, out of sight, with a noise like a bonfire raging. Then white water jetted out into shuddering froth, beating upstream and back, then swirled on, gradually subsiding in the stillness of a wide, dark pool.

When the wind blows from the west in Borsley you can hear the motorway, and it goes on all night, a sound between a tremor and a hum. That was the sound that drifted from the far edge of the pool. Low glistening rocks reached in from both banks like two outstretched arms that didn't meet. Between them, still glassy-dark but quivering slightly, was the lip of the waterfall. First we felt it, then we saw it, rising in the half-light: fine mist rising from the drop we couldn't see.

"Hey," said Ben, "be careful." Alia was strides ahead by now. When the path got difficult, she slithered down and jumped. She landed on the flat rock, two metres down, crouching on all fours like a cat. She looked back, mouthing something that was swallowed by the rush of water.

"Alia," Ben called, "wait for us." He and Hugo were clambering down behind her, as she hopped out lightly on to the last low rock at the lip of the fall. Dark water lapped along it, picking up speed, white streaks appearing in it as the river gathered for its leap.

"No!" Hugo shouted. She was poised at the edge now, flexing her knees, with her gaze fixed on the rock opposite. How far was it? Three metres? Four? Now I was shouting too, though she couldn't have heard – "Alia, don't!" – as she swung her arms slightly, rocking her body back and forwards, closer to the point of no return. "No!" shouted Hugo again. Then she turned and looked at him, eyes glinting.

"Not now," Hugo said quietly. "You'll fly ... on that stage tonight."

She looked at him, eye to eye, a minute. Then she said, "Give me your knife." I could see Hugo hesitate, but that gaze of hers was on him. He reached inside his jacket. The glint of the knife.

Alia shook out the band that had tied back her hair, arching her head back so her whole pale neck was bare. She lifted the knife and with three swift carvings hacked away the flounce of hair. She held it aloft, the way a Celtic warrior might have held a newly severed head. Then she stretched out her arm above the gush of the fall, and let it go. The hair was gone before it hit the water.

Alia turned to us, laughing. "There, I'm lighter!" she said. Down in the darkening woods, an owl whooo'd.

"Let's get there and show them," she said. "Let's fly."

As we climbed up the bank I caught Ben's eye, or maybe he caught mine. Did I imagine it, or did that look of his say, *Help me*? Right or wrong, that's what I thought, and though I didn't speak, I knew what I was going to do.

17

"Don't worry," I said, "it's a short-cut."
The lane narrowed and narrowed again, till it was a track between overgrowing hedges. Everyone was breathing faster – Ben and Alia and Clive and me. Hugo had gone on ahead, to fix things. He'd be waiting for us at the performers' gate with the guy – one of Jed Alexander's crew – who'd get us in. "He owes me a favour, from way back," said Hugo, and we didn't ask him to explain.

He'd be waiting there already. "Get a move on, Emod," Ben said. "We're meant to be on in half an hour."

"No sweat," I said, sweating.

"Emod..." Alia's voice was as cold as a knife blade, just behind my neck. "If we don't make it, if we're late..." She drew in a long slow breath. "You know everything hangs on this, don't you? I mean *everything*..."

"I'm doing my best," I said. "The van…"

We were well off the main road now, and no houses in sight. It was near enough dusk that I could see the pale glow from the festival lights behind the hill, making sharp silhouettes of a couple of trees. You could almost believe it really was a short-cut. One thing was sure: nobody would be just happening to pass by. I gave it a couple of sharp bends more, then wrenched the gear-stick straight from second to reverse. The engine gave a grating yelp, choked, shuddered and came to a stop. "Christ," said Ben, "what's happened?"

I was climbing out already. "The idiot stalled her," Clive said, "that's all. Just start up again."

I had the bonnet open. "No," I called back, "something went, I'm sure it did. Someone get a torch." That gave me a moment. Before Clive came up with torch in hand, I'd reached deep in the guts of the engine, found the wire I knew would be crucial and ripped it out with one swift tug.

"Can't see a problem…" Clive was squinting in. "Try her again, Ben." Ben turned the ignition. Nothing. Absolutely nothing. Alia was scrambling out, her movements quick and jerky, close to panic. Without looking round, I tossed the wire deep in the hedge behind me, while I tried to arrange my face into a look of shock. *That's it, folks*, I was thinking. *We ain't going nowhere.* They would thank me one day, if I ever told them. But for now it was the end of Transformer, the whole crazy story. And good riddance, I thought. That was that.

"Do something!" Alia hissed.

"I'm trying, aren't I? Hold that torch still…" I plunged my head into the engine, doing my best imitation of a Formula One pit-stop mechanic. I made sure I got smeared with oil all over, so I looked the part. Alia's gaze was on my back, I could feel it like a knife between the shoulder blades.

"We've blown it," said Clive. "Busted. Screwed."

"Hugo'll help," Ben said feebly.

"Not if he can't find us. This is Emod's short-cut, remember? Did you tell him, Emod?"

"Well…" I said.

Alia was quivering. She looked pale and jagged. Savage. "Do something, somebody!" she said again.

Clive shoved me aside. "Here, let me try. You're useless." He rammed his arm in deep under the fan belt and ferreted. After a moment he paused, the flicker of a question on his face.

"Funny…" he said. Then Alia screamed. It wasn't the curse-hiss that she'd used on Mary Field, more an animal squeal, like something in a snare, of rage and pain. At the same time there was a snarl from the engine, which couldn't be happening, because that vital bit of wire was over the hedge in a bramble patch, I'd seen to that. So it couldn't be happening that the engine suddenly fired, but it did. Clive staggered back as if he'd been kicked. He was clutching his hand. There was blood. "Ben, you stupid *bastard*," he screamed, "you nearly got my fingers…"

157

In the cab, Ben held his hands up. "Didn't touch it," he said, "honest!" But the engine was throbbing and ready to go. Alia was motionless, her cropped hair standing up in spikes like a little girl waking from a nightmare, but her eyes were calm and sure. Clive was yelling at Ben; Ben was shaking his head, protesting; I just stood there thinking: *this isn't happening*.

"Let's get on with it," said Alia, in control. "Ten minutes … we've got time."

In the dusk, the lights that played on the canvas awning made the stage bloom like a huge exotic flower. Patterns of purple, lime and puce rotated and flickered in beat with the music – an old Jed Alexander single – that pulsed from the towers of speakers, several times head-high. From the performers' gate I looked through the wire and glimpsed them, happy kids dressing up wild for the weekend, faces mixed up with balloons and banners and dribbles of smoke, all lit up with the warm reflected multi-coloured glow. Why couldn't I be out there with them, just watching, thinking it was just a show?

It was 10.25. Hugo's man at the gate was a pot-bellied roadie, balding on top though a few strands of greasy tangle still flopped in his eyes. He blinked all the time, and he dished us out our backstage passes fast, without looking, though he kept one eye on Hugo all the time. What did Hugo have on him,

I wondered, thinking of the footnote in the book. He didn't look like a long-lost mate to me. He was simply afraid. He nodded to the Day-Glo-jacketed security men. They waved us through.

Backstage, in the artists' enclosure, was another world. From behind, you could see that the flickering canopy above the stage was sheets of canvas, lashed with hawsers. High over our heads, the speaker towers stalked tall as the Martians in *War of the Worlds*, in the dazzling aura of their own lights. The stage was a matrix of scaffolding poles, clamped into towers, hiding hollow spaces, just like any building site. Beer cans already littered the dead place under the stage, where sheaves of cables trailed down, out to generators in the darkness, throbbing quietly out of sight.

"Get ready to get up there fast!" Hugo whispered. "Just plug into the amps up there. They're ten times bigger than yours," he added for Clive. Alia was clutching the shaman drum against her chest like a child with her teddy, but her eyes were fixed and bright. "Give Emod and me two minutes to get to the mixing desk," said Hugo. "When you hear the PA go down, move!" He ducked under the stage, then looked back. "You might only get the chance for one number," he said, "so make it the big one. Play it as if it's the last thing you'll ever do." I ducked after him, running almost bent double, tripping and stumbling on cables. A security man looked up when we slipped out under the front of the stage but we flashed him our passes and he waved us over to the little fenced-off cockpit in the front rows of the crowd.

There was somebody there, the next band's sound-man maybe, but I'll give it to Hugo, he didn't even break his stride. As the man looked up and round, Hugo bent down as if to whisper something, and the rabbit-punch landed so smoothly that you'd have thought it was one can of lager too many made him crumple to the ground. Then Hugo had the headphones on, was in the seat, was in control. His hands skittered over the dials and switches. He had tapes of our samples laid out, slotted in position. "Now, Jed Alexander..." he said through his teeth, and cut the record in mid-song.

In the sudden hush, the amps hummed, ready. There were Clive and Ben, moving in the shadows, and Alia, stepping forward into the white light, not much more than a shadow herself, very small and thin between the ziggurats of speakers. Above her, the canopy of canvas rippled in a gust of sluggish wind. Even as she stepped forward her hand was coaxing the shaman drum into a rhythm: *thrumm ... thrumm...* Clive's bass line was in place, very quietly, but as Hugo's hands played on the switches, both sounds swelled like distant, but approaching, thunder, sending ripples through the crowd. He picked up a mike and jacked a socket. "Now..." His voice reverberated through the music. "A band you'll never forget. *Transformer!* Courtesy of Klaus

Productions. Jed, this one's for you!" And he slammed up the volume as they hit the first verse, *Real Time*, dead on cue.

stars and ice, my soul in flight
ride the wind and moon tonight

Ben was playing high harmonics, ghost notes forming out of nowhere. Clive took his bass down to a rattling throb, like a moth with metal wings, bumping the window, trying to get in at the light. There was another sound too. Almost silent at first, Hugo had slotted a sample: that low gasping rasping shaman voice. He was bringing the volume of it up, so slowly you wouldn't have noticed it at all until suddenly it filled your head and lungs and bones.

you can't hear or touch or see
capture, judge, imprison me

A few fat drops of rain were falling, but no one noticed. No one was dancing or swaying their arms or anything; they were hypnotized, watching Alia, hanging on the next note. Only Hugo wasn't watching. He had his head down, locked in his dials and monitors like an airline pilot flying on instruments, flying blind. He was bringing the volume up steadily, like the roar of engines, till it hurt, and we weren't at the climax yet, not by a long way. I thought of a film I saw once when a suicidal pilot aimed his jet straight at a mountain, and as the engines screamed and the passengers screamed louder, he had had that same look in his eyes...

one last jump and I'll fly free
into Real Time

There was a surge in the crowd, people fighting their way forward. For a moment I thought we had another scuffle, like at the club. But no, there were helmets: the police... For once, the music helped them. The crowd jostled back vaguely, but didn't turn round. The jeering began as the security barrier parted and a couple of constables vaulted on to the stage. One pulled Clive's plug and Clive swung towards him, raising his bass like a battleaxe, and Ben lost his fingering on a high riff and swung around to face them too.

Only Alia hadn't moved. From the first, she had clung to the microphone stand, as if her legs might give way any moment, and she pulled it closer as the tension mounted, eyes shut, lips just an inch from the mike. Now there was only her voice above that ghost-breath chanting, but she didn't seem to know she was alone up there. She swayed a little, clinging to the stand as if she might start dancing with it, and suddenly it was Death and the Maiden from a medieval woodcut, with a young girl swaying, swirling with her arms round a skeleton's waist.

There was a crackling and a moan of feedback, and the first hard drops of rain began to fall. Maybe one of them hit Alia and jogged her from her trance, because she looked up, looked around her as if she was waking from a dream ... and looked down.

She must have seen the police and security men,

all scrambling towards her. Certainly she saw her parents, with a woman PC. Maybe she even caught sight of the bodyguards shoving a path through the crowd for a runt of a man in flash gear, waving his arms: *Get them off!* That was Jed Alexander. Maybe all that she saw, like an illumination, was the certain fact that everything – the band, the song, the night, the sky – was coming crashing round our ears, as she pulled herself up to her full height, stretched out her arm in that cursing gesture and…

I leaped at the desk as Hugo threw the volume to MAX. He must have sensed the movement because he met me, twisted round and lashed out with fists and feet. My hand raked among the switches, missed the volume and cut the stage into darkness, as the feedback howled out like a huge and lonely wolf.

And Alia screamed her scream.

18

If it was lightning, like they said afterwards, why wasn't there thunder? Or maybe it was drowned by the screech of all the amps before they blew?

The world went pearl-white for an instant, so bright that it hurt, with no shadows, only the bare bones of the stage and towers etched brighter than the background that was blinding anyway. Before I could shield my eyes there was darkness, full of flashes and after-images. No, they were real: streamers of sparks fell, crackling, as one of the lighting towers staggered and lurched to a terrible angle. I could hear the rising wail of panic, like a pressure cooker coming to the boil, as the crowd tried to scatter. Black speaker boxes big as wardrobes were slithering off their mountings, avalanching down; cables snapped and lashed with sparks still trailing, like electric whips above the fleeing crowd, and falling spotlights burst with sick thuds and a splintering of glass.

Then it was dark, until the first flames started fingering the canvas of the stage. The rain came on hard now, thick lukewarm drops like melting butter, and it sizzled on the burning awning, sending up billows of smoke that gradually turned orange as the fire took hold. Silhouetted against it, I saw figures teetering, jumping from the stage as if on the deck of the sinking *Titanic*. I saw the shapes of policemen, gathering survivors in a huddle on the ground.

"Where's Alia?" I said when I reached them. There was Ben, staring dumbly, wincing, as a St John's Ambulance man pressed a damp cloth to his arm. There was a scorch-mark, maybe worse; I didn't want to know. "Where's Dee?" he muttered at me, but he didn't really see me. "Where's Dee?" There was Clive, turning to look at the wreck of the stage as two security men tried to coax him away. "Please leave the field in an orderly fashion," coughed an ancient megaphone voice, again and again. A few whoops of a siren cleared a path through the scattering bleating flocks of people, and an ambulance nudged through, its blue light strobing like the thing bands always do on stage. It came straight past, waved on by security men with messages crackling on their walkie-talkies, to a more urgent call than us. "Where's Alia?" I said but no one answered, though I said it again and again.

There was a huddle of tents at the back of the artists' enclosure and that's where they let us lie down in the mud. Lit by flames, it might have been a refugee encampment. What was left of the crowd was filing out now, panic over, with their heads down like a defeated army, sodden in the rain. Alia's parents gazed at me as though they might speak. They didn't, but the things they might have said – *How could you…? Why didn't you…? Why…?* – went on and on inside my mind.

"Where's Alia?" The fire engines had moved in. No sign of her yet, the WPC said tactfully. Later on they'd search the wreckage of the stage.

No, I thought. No, she's not dead. Somehow, if she was, I'd know.

And then the other thought … *Where's Hugo?*

"I need the loo," I said, struggling upright. The moment I was out of sight, behind the tent, I cut into the straggling column of the crowd. As we crushed through the gate, someone tugged at my arm. It was one of the hitchers from earlier, and her face was smudged with mud and tears. "Have you seen Mandy?" she wailed. "My friend Mandy, you know…"

"Sorry," I said. "Don't worry, she'll be OK."

"Help me search, please!"

"Sorry." I prised her fingers off my arm as gently as I could. "I'm looking for somebody too…"

"If it's that singer of yours, she's gone."

Stopping dead in a moving crowd isn't easy. Now it was me who grabbed her arm. "When? Which way? Who with? Are you sure?"

"I wouldn't mistake her, would I?" said the girl. "She looked dead scared. She ran off on her own, across the field, that way…"

Just then there was the sharp cough of an engine. A motorbike engine. Hugo's. Once, twice, three times it coughed and wouldn't fire. Then it growled into life. "Hey!" the Brummie girl wailed as I let go her arm. "What about Mandy?" But I was fighting my way through the crowd. Hugo's motorbike snarled, impatient, stop-start through the crush, then revved. I caught a glimpse of his face, impassive even now, beneath the helmet, as he swerved off.

I made for the van.

It took me a while to get free of the crowds. Where would Alia run to? Certainly not home, not Borsley. "I'm never going back," she'd said. *Across the field … that way…* Where was there, but the cottage? And it was across the fields, that way…

And Hugo? He'd paid off his grudge against Jed Alexander; he didn't need us now, unless … unless he wanted more. Unless he wanted Alia, body and soul.

I was cutting through the dark lanes fast, watching for corners, not thinking of much except getting there, so I almost missed it. Down by the bridge, by the Horan's Leap footpath, leaning in the brambles was a black shape. I backed up and looked again. Yes, Hugo's bike.

It was no time for parking. I left the van there in

the road. Of course, I should have known. Hugo wasn't a stranger to this valley; he'd have known where Alia would come out, making for Horan's Place, if she cut across the fields. She'd have dropped into the woods somewhere near here, avoiding the road if she had any sense, but she had to cross the river at the bridge. So all he had to do was wait.

The wood was hushed but full of small sounds. Now the storm had passed over big drops fell from wet leaves heavily, like something moving in the undergrowth, stop-start, here and there. The rush of the water was louder, swollen by the rain. The owl we heard earlier called again, further down the valley. As I looked from the parapet the clouds began to thin and break up, and a scatter of moonlight caught the branches, making the shadows beneath seem even deeper and more dark. Far below, the foam on the pool was a white glow, though the pool itself was blackness, and the spray from the waterfall a faint smudge on the air.

There was no sign of Hugo. So I started down the path.

It was steep mud, deceptive and greasy, and I slipped straight away and stayed down, moving in a slither on all fours. Suddenly I dug my fingers in the mud and tensed there. Something moved, just below me. Still in a crouch, I looked down, and saw Hugo stand up, with his face in moonlight, profile like an Easter Island statue, looking down the valley, not at me.

I followed his gaze, and there was a movement in the bushes. There was Alia, picking her way along the hillside through the trees. As Hugo made his move towards her I shouted, but it was lost in the sound of the river and I don't know if he heard. She looked up, though, and as she looked she saw him. For a moment in the moonlight, like a rabbit in the headlights of a car, she froze. Then she ducked off the path, slipped and went slithering down. She missed her footing as she landed, sprawled a moment, then pulled herself upright on the wide flat stone. Behind her, the dark pool trembled as it gathered for the fall.

Hugo came to the top of the bank above her and they met each other's eyes. He stretched out his arms in a dumb-show of a bear-hug. Alia took a step back, shaking her head. Her mouth mimed *No!* Hugo climbed down the bank, very slowly, keeping his eyes on her, step by step. Then they were both on the rock, a few metres between them, as he took a pace on, and paused, and she took a pace back, and their mouths moved and the words were swallowed by the waterfall. Finally, as her last pace took her to the very edge, he smiled.

I was shouting, I guess, from the way that my throat hurt, but Alia and Hugo couldn't hear. Even without the sound of the water, they would have been together in a world I couldn't reach. Between me and them, the pool lay, dangerously still.

My fingers had tightened on something in the

mud beside me, something hard. A rock. I tugged it up, struggled to my feet and slipped again but as I slipped I hurled it. When I looked again, they had both turned, and in the second it took for Hugo to take in what had happened – splash in the water … a stone … who threw it … someone in the bushes … me – Alia turned to face the Leap. An impossible jump, from a standing start on wet stones on to wet stones, too far even in the dry, without the drop… But Alia leaped.

One foot skidded as she landed and slipped back. The rush of the water clutched at her ankle as her arms lunged forwards grabbing as if there was something she just might get hold of in the air. For a second she teetered, on the point of balance, then jerked forwards as if something pulled her, something not in the laws of physics. She sprawled full length on the glistening stone.

Hugo stared, with Horan's Leap between them. It could have been three miles, not metres. Alia got to her feet, slowly, and turned to look back at him. Her face, pale as the moon, was wide and white, with round enormous eyes of darkness. Owl face. She lifted her arms and they were broad white wings, outstretched.

Then she was scrambling up the far bank, just a scared girl, running, and Hugo turned, as if he'd just remembered me. He raised a hand and clenched it slowly, as if the sheer force of hate could pull me down the slope towards him, then he was climbing towards me. I flipped round on to all fours, dug my fingers in, grabbed at brambles, nettles, anything to keep me scrambling upwards; I slipped, gained inches, slipped back, got hold of a slimy root, and heaved. I heard his breathing just below me as my hands reached the parapet and I scrabbled at it, kicking one leg over. Then I was upright on the tarmac, running for the van.

Hugo's hands appeared on the parapet as I stabbed the key in the ignition, and turned it. Nothing. Turned it. Nothing. Hugo's head appeared. Whatever Alia had done to fix it earlier, whatever impossible thing, it had worn off somehow. Then, as if at the thought of Alia, it fired.

As Hugo loomed up on the bridge, I rammed the gear-stick in and the van shot forward. He jumped back, sprawling on the low wall as my front wing gouged into it, raising a shower of sparks, just where his legs had been. He could have jumped at the bonnet or wrestled the door but he hesitated, just a second, and I crunched the gear-stick to reverse. As the van skittered back the corner of my eye caught something. Hugo's motorbike. With a wrench of the wheel I slewed the Transit into it with a dustbin-rolling clang. My back doors buckled and burst inwards as we hit the wall square on, and bits of the bike were thrown aside. I jolted into first as Hugo staggered at me, like a bear on hind legs, and the van jumped forward, missing him by inches as he threw himself aside.

There was a clattering from somewhere near the axle, and a worrying hiss from the engine, but I wasn't going to stop and check. Hugo lurched upright behind me, staring baffled for a moment, then he vanished. The bonnet was leaking steam now steadily, but I put my foot down, chancing the bends, because I knew where he would head next. Just where Alia would be going, unless I could reach her first. To Horan's Place.

19

"Alia?"

The house was silent. Door locked, windows dark and somehow smaller than they'd ever been, as if it shut its eyes to sleep. "Alia, are you in there?" We'd come all this way from the Green Room, and I was still asking the same question. Just like that night, there was no answer.

Halfway down the track, the van had packed up. With a last hiss of steam, the engine seized up and I free-wheeled down the last bit, lurching on each bend. One tyre at least had gone down; I could hear the wheel hub grating on the stones. I came to a rest slewed across the last corner, and I killed the one headlight. As I slipped out, I reached under the seat and closed my fingers round the cool shaft of the wheel brace. Just in case.

There was a patch of bluish moonlight, like an empty stage, in front of Horan's Place. On one side, the woods kept their secrets; on the other, the cottage hunkered in the shadow of the overhang.

"Alia? It's only me, it's Emod."

The words hung in the air a little longer than they ought to, between the house and the rock face, with a hollow sound. I read about a tribe once who never say their names aloud. If an enemy knows what your name is, he can go and shout it in the forest, so the spirits hear. Then they can get in to your soul.

Could Alia be in the cottage? Did she have a key? No, only Hugo would have one; he'd make sure that he was in control.

He couldn't have got here that fast, could he? The steep slippery path up the valley with the boulders and brambles, in the dark. No, that was impossible. But had Alia made it? Was she stumbling through the woods now, lost, for Hugo to find her? Would I have to go into the forest and look?

Then I knew that somebody was watching me.

As I looked up, the corner of my eye caught a hint of a movement, as slight as if a wind had stirred the shadow of one leaf. But there was no wind, no movement at all. The valley was echoey quiet, like a studio about to go on air. Something had ducked out of sight behind the end wall. I edged towards the corner, wheel brace lifted, back against the wall.

"Come out," I said shakily. "I want to help you."

The shadow that stepped out was shorter than I'd expected, shorter and wider. Mary Field.

At the sight of the wheel brace she flinched. Both hands went up, like a child nabbed by the teacher saying, *Not me, sir!* I stared stupidly. All I could find to say was, "You…?"

She looked at me, calm now, for some while. Then she nodded. "You can put that down, son. No need to be frit of me."

"You…?" I tried again. "Are you … all right?"

She almost smiled. "Don't you worry 'bout me," she said. "Tough old bird, this one. It's that poor child you should be feared for."

"Poor child? You mean Alia?"

"Who else? Poor starved thing, she's in torment."

"But … but she hurt you."

"Not her. She didn't do it. It's the thing inside, the thing that eats her, that's what did it. Her, she's just a child."

Then both of us turned. There was a sound in the woods, very quiet but not far away. It was almost a bird cry and almost a small thing in pain, an injured hedgehog maybe, snuffling and squealing, but somehow we knew it wasn't either. By the time we got to the edge of the bank, where the footpath climbed out of the woods, we caught sight of Alia, some way below, there for a moment in a patch of moonlight, then gone, but we could hear her, weeping softly as she came.

The bank almost defeated her. She slipped and gave way, struggled to her feet and slipped again. She gained a little ground on hands and knees, then slumped, clinging on to a tree root, sobbing. As we reached down to help her she lifted her face with an effort, too tired to be surprised or frightened. The moonlight was full on it, pitiless and cold. It was almost the face in the Green Room mirror, the moment before the skin began to peel away. Not quite, because she wasn't smiling.

As we helped her up, she staggered. We propped her up between us, and it wasn't hard, she had so little weight. Close up, there was a sharp smell to her skin that I'd noticed before and thought was some strange perfume – almost chemical, the way I imagine embalming fluid might be.

"I'm sorry," she said faintly. "I never meant to... All those people. And Ben..." She shuddered. "He was the last one I wanted to hurt..."

"He'll be OK," I said. "You're the one who needs help."

There was another sound, a heavier crunching, from deep in the woods. "Oh God," I said, "that's Hugo." I looked at Mary Field. She understood. "There must be somewhere..." I thought of the house. Locked. The van? Its back doors hanging open and the engine dead. "The spring," said Mary Field. "She'd be safe in there."

The padlock and chain on the lean-to didn't give at first, but on the third or fourth heave with the wheel brace they sprang apart with a sharp chink. As I fumbled for matches and candle inside, Mary Field was already easing Alia into the dark. I slid the bolt, and as the candle flared up, saw how flimsy it was, one iron bolt attached by rusty screws to mouldy wood. I grabbed old planks, oil cans, stones, a rake, a bucket, anything, and wedged them as tight as I could against the door.

There was only one candle. I handed it to Mary Field, and Alia followed her, dumb and vaguely compliant, like she'd never been before. They ducked through the cleft in the rock and I was in the dark. A blurry trace of moonlight came through the crack beneath the door.

A shadow moved over it and blocked it. It was horrible how softly he could move, for all his bulk. And how soft his voice was when he called in, "Alia ... my bird. I knew I'd find you here." He tried the door. He pushed it, he rattled the handle.

"Don't be afraid," he purred, but I could hear his breathing stiffen. "Just open the door." A pause. "You need me," he said in a different voice. "Nobody else will help you now."

"You're wrong about that," I said, and wished I hadn't. Too late now. I heard him smile.

"Well, well," he said. "Young Emod..."

"She's not here," I tried.

"Don't waste my time," he said. "I can *feel* she's in there. I know everything about her. I'm her only friend."

"Friend!" I said. "I saw you at the waterfall. She could have killed herself."

"Better to die," he said calmly, "than to waste a

gift like hers." He gave the door a hard shove. "Open this door, Emod. Open it now and I won't hurt you. Just let me have Alia, and you won't see us again."

He must have been poised, his shoulder ready, all the time it took me to gather my breath, try once to speak, moisten my lips and force the word out: "No." The second it left my lips the door shuddered. Oil cans clattered from the barricade, the rake handle splintered, but the bolt didn't quite give way. There was a crack between two planks now, I could see the light through. Something prised into the crack and levered; there was a splintery sound and as the moonlight caught it I saw the blade of Hugo's knife.

"Emod," he said in his soft voice, "you're a reasonable man. Let me speak to her. You'll see: she won't say no."

"Eff off, Hugo," I said. Then the door came down.

He must have taken a run up this time. The planks that had made up the door just ripped apart, and he came straight through. The junk I'd piled up so carefully scattered like litter in a high wind. I threw myself back and grabbed the first thing that felt like a weapon, and as I edged back towards the cleft into the cave I realized I had the rake handle. It had splintered at just the right angle, with a slightly jagged sharp point at the end. Holding it the way I imagined a Stone Age hunter might have held his spear with a cave bear coming down on him, I backed into the cave.

Mary Field looked up in the light of the candle. She didn't ask me to explain. I waited for Hugo's first arm to appear in the crack in the rock, then I stabbed with the handle as hard as I could. A roar of pain, that could have been a bear or tiger, filled the cave.

"Damn you," he said. "You know, don't you, she's mine. Nothing's going to keep her from me. Nothing on earth."

"He's right." It was Alia's voice, hardly a whisper. "You can't stop him. Let me go out to him. He won't hurt you then."

I don't swear much, usually, but I did it again.

Hugo was in the cleft, I could hear. I got ready to stab. But this time when the arm appeared it had something around it – the oilcloth I'd seen out there in the lean-to, wrapped around and around to make a shield. I stabbed once, twice, three times but it glanced off. Hugo was crouching down, shielding himself; he was half the way through. I grabbed the candle and thrust it at the oilcloth. It caught at once, as if there was petrol on it and a rush of smoke caught at my throat, and I was coughing, choking so hard that I almost didn't notice Hugo's roaring as he flapped and struggled backwards, wrestling the flames off his arm.

Then we heard the cars. The voices. The police cars couldn't have got past the van, but that was enough to tell them something was happening, and then they would have heard the cries and seen the smoke. There was a megaphone voice shouting something. Suddenly there was just a quiet flicker from the oily rags outside the entrance, and Hugo was gone.

Alia was lying on the cave floor now. Mary Field had dipped in the little font under the back wall and was dabbing cool water gently on Alia's forehead. "The water of life..." she muttered. Softly, Alia sobbed.

"We'll get you to a doctor," I said. Alia shook her head. For the third time that evening, I said the f-word. I didn't care if this cave was some kind of sacred place. "You're ill," I said. "Even I can see that. Nothing mystical or magical or anything. You just haven't been eating, that's all."

In a far-off way, rather terribly, she smiled. "Oh, yes," she said. "I've overcome all that. I haven't eaten for a month. Isn't that wonderful?"

"No!" I screamed. "It's sick. You ought to be in hospital."

She lifted her head painfully, and turned to Mary Field. "I want to stay here," she whispered. "For ever."

Mary Field shook her head. "No," she said, "it's the water of life, not death. You got it wrong. Poor child."

As they helped us out into the night air through the

wreckage of the door, I looked at the sergeant. "Where is he?" I said.

"Who?" said the sergeant.

"Hugo… He was in here." A cold creeping feeling had settled on my skin, and it wasn't just the cool night air. "You had him cornered. There isn't another way out."

The sergeant just looked at me. Shock: that was what he'd be thinking. "You just take it easy. Tell us later," he said.

As they led us out behind the house, I twisted away and looked back. "The shed roof," I said. "If he got up there…"

Over the roof of the lean-to, the overhang jutted out, crumbling. The policeman looked at it and smiled.

"Huh," he said drily, as if it was a good joke. "What did he do: fly?"

20

"Come with me," said the doctor, leading the way with brisk, clipped steps. "You must be worried about your wee friend." There was something about her Edinburgh accent that felt sharp and clean, like the tang of hospital disinfectant in the air.

Out of the third-floor window was a cloudy sky, and under that lay Borsley, busy and boring as usual. It had got us back after all, even Alia, and it had never even noticed we had gone.

"Oh," I said, "everyone worries about Alia." Our footsteps echoed down the corridor. "Looks like she's got the place to herself."

"We're a bit short staffed," said the doctor, "but don't worry, we're still here for emergencies."

"Is Alia an emergency? Is it serious?"

The doctor stopped us, her hand on the door

marked CROWLEY WARD, but she didn't open it. "The way your friend was going on," she said, "she could have collapsed at any moment."

"She fainted once or twice," I said.

"I mean: collapsed and died."

The clock on the wall above us gave a loud *tunk* in the silence and the minute hand jerked on. "But ... she's OK now, isn't she?"

"She's not out of the woods by any means. We've got a drip up, just to stop her dehydrating. And we're doing blood checks hourly. The electrolytes go haywire, in severe starvation."

"That's what it is," I said, "just starvation?"

"Not just starvation. *Anorexia nervosa*. These poor lassies... There's so many of them nowadays." So that was Alia, I thought, just one of *these poor lassies ... so many of them*. And she thought she was so special.

"There's one thing I don't understand." That was a joke – there were hundreds, but most of them a doctor couldn't answer. "If she was so weak all this time, how come she seemed ... so strong?"

"Endorphins," said the doctor simply. "When a body is starving, the brain gives them a shot of this chemical that gives you energy – so they can go out and hunt for food, I suppose. Also it dulls the pain. Just one of those things Mother Nature does to keep us going." She gave a professional smile. "Shall we go in now?"

*　　*　　*

"Emod," said Alia without opening her eyes. There were deep grey shadows round them as if she had been punched. She looked limp and small in a kind of cot with metal bars on either side. The sheets were rucked up round her. "I can't get comfortable," she said. "It hurts. They've put things in my arm." The skin looked bruised and blue around the dressing, where the spike was strapped in. A clear plastic tube looped up to a bag of fluid, where a digital counter ticked off drips per minute.

"Clever stuff," I said, for something to say.

"I'll tell you a secret," she said. "I tried to switch that thing off, you know the way I can, by thinking…"

"Don't talk like that," I said. "You'll be OK now."

"*OK!*" She roused, just a shade of the old fierce Alia. "*OK*'s no good to me. Don't worry, though. I couldn't do it. I can't do it any more." She was looking at me as if she was accusing me of something, with those eyes like bruises. I tried to read the thin red numbers on the digital display, but they kept blurring. Must be a mechanical fault. I don't cry.

"What a mess," I said. "Look at you. Look at … it all."

She winced. "Ben … how is he?"

"He'll heal. Not too many scars."

"What about … the festival?" I looked away. "Please, Emod, they won't tell me what happened. Was anybody … you know?"

"Jed Alexander's off the danger list, it said in the paper. But he might not play guitar again. As for the kids in the crowd…"

Alia lay limply, staring at the ceiling. "Poor things. I never meant to…" she said.

"It was an accident," I said. "Freak weather conditions. Act of God." The last phrase seemed a bad joke. "You're not to blame," I said. "It's Hugo."

"Hugo! Have you heard anything?"

"They haven't caught him, if that's what you mean. Don't worry, they will."

"They won't," said Alia, letting her eyes close. "He told me he'd come to me … whatever happened." The small ward was quiet, almost empty. Outside the window a starling perched on the fire-escape, making a noise like a fingernail down a blackboard.

"You've got to start eating again," I said.

She shuddered as if something nasty had touched her. Her eyes opened wearily. "You don't get it, do you? I nearly made it. I was nearly perfect. Nearly special. Nearly … *wonderful*. If I can't be that … why be anything?" She sank her head back in the pillow. Tight lines round her mouth and eyes, shrunken cheeks… I remembered my aunt, near the end, when she was really ill, I mean *really* ill, the kind of illness that just comes and gets you, not the kind you ask in for yourself. And then I snapped.

"OK! You're not! You're not special at all. Very ordinary, just another boring ugly anorexic, just like

185

all the others." She rolled her head away. The ward door had opened and a nurse strode in. I suppose I was shouting, but I didn't care. "Bloody Dying Swan routine! You've got everyone running round after you, haven't you? Always have had. *We're so worried about Alia...* Yeah, well, I've had it, I've had it right up to here!"

The doctor's hand was on my shoulder, steering me gently, firmly back towards the door. "You know what I mean, Alia," I called back. "You're a coward. You're just afraid to be ... to be ordinary. Bit of a mess, like the rest of us. Like me!" I braced my arms against the doorpost. "Well?" I said.

She lifted her head a little, to look past the nurse who had moved in between us. "Emod," she said faintly, "come and see me again."

"Not till morning, dear," the nurse said.

"Don't go away," Alia said, with an effort. "Please stay, just in case." *In case what?* I would have asked her, but the doctor gave a final official shove. The door shut with a click.

"Professionally," said the doctor tartly, "I would tell you to go home and get a good night's sleep. On the other hand..." Her ice-grey eyes creased at the corners. "I'd say she means it. There are soft chairs in the waiting room."

Some time in the small hours the rain came, sweeping out of the west, maybe from Cornwall, and the windows shuddered with it. It drowned out all the thoughts and fear and worries and at last I fell asleep.

A wind blew in the dream, too, over wastes of Arctic tundra, whipping up the fine snow till I couldn't see the join between earth and sky. Something was crying, though at first I couldn't say if it was the wind, or something alive somewhere out in the cold. It came nearer, a wavering cry that tracked past once then veered back, hunting. Maybe hunting me.

Then a flurry of snow whirled at me and in it the wings flared and the owl hung there in front of me, yellow eyes glaring, claws out-flexed, its beak open to scream. Then it banked in the wind and let the blizzard take it, planing out into endless winter. *Lonely, lonely* ... it seemed to cry. And it circled round to strike again.

This time it whacked past so close I could feel its wing-beat. I could see a gout of dried blood on its beak. Of course it longed for warm blood, I could see that now. How else could it live in this wasteland but by killing? *Lonely, hungry*... And the wind beat round us, thudding like a drum, a wide skin drum where thin stick-figures of people, birds and beasts were mapped out like the prey's tracks in the snow.

It swooped back a third time, spring-loaded its talons and dropped. But not on me. Somewhere close by came a scream. Then I was lying there, cramped, heart thudding, struggling to wake up on the waiting room floor.

Owl. Alia. Alia. Owl.

Still staggering with sleepiness, I raced upstairs. CROWLEY WARD. The door flapped behind me as I barged through and the night nurse looked up from her Stephen King paperback, blinking. I was already halfway down the ward. The curtains were drawn round Alia's bed, but the way they were moving... As I ripped them back I saw the dark shape crouched as if it had landed there, just inside the window, which was open, letting in the sound and smell of rain.

His face was motionless as ever, and more than ever like a carving of a spirit-guide, half man, half bird-beast, on a totem pole. It had been his hair, maybe, that let him pass as just a beat-up one-time hippy, but now that disguise had been stripped from him. Half the hair was scorched off; exposed, the skin glistened with purplish burns. The other half was shaved, and the stubble glowed like frost with fine droplets of rain.

Hugo brought up the knife and let it flash between us, then let it fall to horizontal, just in front of Alia's throat. She was locked in the crook of his left arm, not protesting, limp and stiff as a marionette with her strings cut. A loose hospital nightie rode up round the knobs of bone that were her knees. She tugged at the drip tube vaguely. With a glint, the blade sliced through the plastic and it flicked back. In the silence, clear solution dribbled on the floor.

"That's right," said Hugo. The blade quivered closer, almost grazing her throat, and she leaned back, nestling her head in his shoulder.

"Alia," I said. "Don't let him."

Hugo smiled. It had never come easy to him, smiling. Now it creased his burnt skin; I could see it gave him pain. "The knife is for your benefit only. She is coming of her own free will."

"She isn't," I said. "Alia, say no!"

He looked at me like some schoolteachers do, too weary to be bitter. "How could you possibly know?" he said. "How could you know what *she* wants, a dull commonplace soul like you." As he spoke, he eased himself to the window, one leg on the sill; a sharp tug and Alia was a life-sized ventriloquist's dummy balanced on his knee.

"I know what *you* want," I said. "*Better dead than waste her gift* ... that's what you said. You just used her. Made her do tricks, like a circus freak."

To my surprise he didn't sneer. He looked straight at me. "Don't you understand?" he said. "I never made Alia do a single thing. I never even taught her. All these powers of hers, they're the powers I'd talked about, read about, yearned, yes, *yearned*, to have ... and never did. Then one night there's a new face in my class. This little girl. And I saw it at once. You can call me a fraud, a charlatan, but grant me this: I knew the real thing when I saw it." His face was shining with rain, his trousers ripped and muddy. Hugo hadn't flown, he hadn't come for her in spirit shape; he'd struggled across fields, through the hospital grounds, out of breath, slipping over in mud, struggling on, like any human being does in desperation.

"Once in a lifetime it comes and I found it. Jed Alexander was just a diversion. An indulgence. Her power, that's the real thing. How can I let your doctors take her, put her back in the cage – *cure* her, they'll call it. Drag her down, when she could *fly*?"

"She'll die," I said. "You'll let her die and you won't care."

He was half out of the window, one leg feeling for the fire-escape. As the cool rain touched her, Alia gave a twitch that might have been a feeble struggle or a groan. "Take my word for it," said Hugo, "deep in her heart, she agrees."

As he eased her out, her thin legs grated on the ledge. He flickered the knife. "If anybody tries to follow..." He straightened up, hoisting her with him. Then the night behind him screamed.

Hugo whipped round and looked up just in time to take the great blur of whiteness, smack, full in the face. A metre wide wing-span was cradling his head for a moment, like a carnival head-dress put on back to front. There were streaks of red spreading out of the whiteness, and the scream had become Hugo's as he clutched to find his face and teetered, and the knife flew up and away as if snatched by the rain.

Alia slid from his grip but I was halfway there already, grabbing her ankle just as it slid from the sill. For a moment Hugo clutched her, more to save himself than to take her, then one foot went out from under him, missing the slippery step and both his hands went up as he toppled, catching the handrail hard in the back so that he cartwheeled. There was a heavy clang and the fire-escape shuddered as he struck it again, three storeys down.

At the same time, or so it seems now, the police car screeched into the car park. I suppose the owl-scream might have been its brakes, or the first whoop of its siren. It's possible that I saw a stray flash of its headlights fanned up through the bars of the fire-escape, and imagined wings. Even the damage to his face, they said later, could have been caused by impact with the metal handrail as he fell.

21

Of course I did go back to visit Alia, in a clinic quite near Borsley. As often, in fact, as I could.

"Emod," she said one day without warning. "Tell me: what's your real name?"

"Don't ask. You'd laugh."

"Can't be funnier than Emod. Try me."

"Promise you won't laugh."

"Promise."

"Well, OK. It's Benedict."

She laughed.

When she'd quite finished and she'd got her breath back, she looked at me straight. "Sorry," she said. "It was your face when you said it. Nothing wrong with Benedict. You could always shorten it to Ben."

"What? How could I? I mean: *Ben* is Ben!"

"So? You've got a right to be who you are, too." I

like that about Alia: she says things like that, things that sound so simple, it's a shock that you've never thought of them before. I might even give it a go. But first, I had a question.

"Alia ... what else did you do when you were, you know, making things happen?"

She thought about it, as if she was adding up an enormous sum. "Nothing," she said.

"Wha-a-at? *Nothing?*"

"That's right. Nothing but the things you saw. And the thing on the fire-escape, how could I have done that? I was hardly conscious." She gave me a curious look. "The only common factor," she said, "is that you were there."

"Uh-oh, wait a minute. Remember: I'm just..."

"...the man with the van. I know, I know," she drummed her fingers.

"Anyway," I said, "logically you're wrong. The common factor is that we were both there, you *and* me."

"Well, well..." she said.

But that's another story.

Also in the Point Horror Unleashed series

BLOOD SINISTER

Celia Rees

Cursed be he who looks inside…

Ellen flipped over to a blank page and then a lot of doodles and a couple of false starts. After an impressive opening, this was beginning to resemble her own diary-keeping. The next solid entry was dated 6th February – almost a month later.

6th February, 1878

The Count is still here but he is grievously ill. Papa is very, very concerned about him. I am as well. That is why I have taken up my diary again; I need someone to talk to.

I have just looked back at my last entries. Papa was right, as usual. The concerns I expressed were groundless. Visiting the Count was not the ordeal I thought it would be. Tom disapproved, as I sensed he would, but, then again, he did volunteer to absent himself from my company. Fransz has proved to be a different but, nevertheless, a charming and fascinating companion. I now look forward to my visits and have seen him nearly every day – which makes his deterioration over the last week or so all the more obvious and all the more distressing.

The night of my first visit, my heart felt full of lead. His apartment is far from ours, down in the depths of the old part of the building. I walked as slowly as possible, hoping it would take a long time to get there. I was surprised that he had been put there instead of in the house as our guest. I said as much to Papa, who replied that it was at his own request and scolded me for dawdling. He was still annoyed with me. Even though I had agreed to do as he asked, there was still bad feeling between us and that made me unhappy; knowing where we were going did not help my mood either. I rarely visit this area. It little resembles the airy wards and well-lit corridors of the upper part of the building.

It is more like a prison than a hospital. Only the most hopeless and difficult patients are kept down here. The attendants are all big burly men who look more like gaolers than nurses. The walls are bare brick. A row of pegs holds the straitjackets used to subdue the patients and everywhere there is the jangle of keys and the slamming of iron on stone as each successive gate is unlocked to allow you through and then locked behind you. The terrible shrieks from some of the cells can be alarming and frightening, but I find the pathetic whimpering and little dry whispers coming from behind certain of the studded iron doors far more distressing. I try to appear indifferent, I am the Doctor's daughter, but being down there makes me nervous.

When we got to the Count's apartments, I was pleasantly surprised. He is living in the oldest part of the building. The room is in the shape of an octagon, the walls are of stone. Pillars support the roof, like in a crypt, and some of them are carved with strange designs. Father told me that scholars believe it to have been built by the Knights Templar for their arcane occult rituals, but no one knows that for sure.

Whatever its original purpose, the room had been transformed from the last time I'd seen it. The Countess has taken a house in Highgate for the duration of her cousin's treatment and she must have scoured every shop in London to provide him with the most comfortable and sumptuous of furnishings. Oil lamps and candles compensate for the lack of natural light and cast a suffused glow over everything. Richly patterned carpets adorn the floors and walls, a heavy brocaded curtain, encrusted with gold and silver thread, cordons off the sleeping quarters. The more public area contains comfortable chairs and sofas. A beautifully carved table holds an exquisite chess set. The Count smiled as we entered and invited me to sit opposite him.

Father left us as we began to play. The board is of marble. The pieces are red and white gold, cool to the touch and incredibly heavy.

"I read of such a thing in a book of your British myths and legends," he told me. "I so liked the idea I had my own set made in Constantinople."

We play. Every night it is the same. I am nervous, because I'm not very good. He is far *superior to me, but he lets me win — some of the time, anyway.*

"Would you like tea?" he asks, after the third or fourth game.

Ivan, his manservant, appears as if from nowhere. Cook is right, he is huge; but so quiet and still, he can be in the room the whole time and you would never notice. He wears the clothes of his country, peasant dress, a loose, coarse-woven woollen tunic, and wide leather belt, over black breeches and knee-length boots. He makes tea in a samovar and we drink it like the Russians from little glasses with no milk. The Count shows me how to suck it through cubed sugar. He offers me tiny cakes, iced and delicious, but takes none himself.

As I eat, he tells me of his home. A land beyond the forests; far, far to the east, at the meeting point of Europe and Asia. And of his castle there, up in the mountains, set on a pinnacle. So high the eagles nest below it, and the mighty river, running at the bottom of the ravine, looks like a thin strip of steel. He talks on and on. I sip my tea and listen. It sounds a wild place, romantic and wonderful...

The first time, Father came to collect me. Other times Ivan accompanies me back to my own quarters. I'm always surprised when it is time to leave. Hours seem to have fled by like so many minutes.

"Again, I have kept you too long. I am so sorry."

He takes my fingers and kisses them. Again, I feel a slight sting on my palm. He turns my hand and kisses it just above the wrist. It is still a queer sensation, but I no longer find it unpleasant.

I have noticed that, when he smiles, he rarely shows his teeth. I find myself glad of it. They are by far his worst feature. If they were otherwise, his looks would be almost perfect. They are not irregular, but they are unusual. The front ones are small, slightly backward sloping, sharp-edged, with tiny serrations. The canines, either side, are large and an odd shape, pointed, almost conical. They are pearly, semi-translucent, more the colour of bone than teeth. No, that analogy is not correct. I have to think about this. The thing they most resemble is the quill of a feather. I glimpsed them tonight, before his full lips shut them off from view. They are like those of another type of creature, something which belongs to a different species altogether. I try not to look at them, but feel compelled to do so. They give me an odd feeling inside as if something were not quite right—

"Ellen. ELLEN! Supper's ready. Are you deaf, child? I've been calling and calling you!"

"Sorry, Gran," she shouted back. "Had my Walkman on. Be there now."

Ellen reluctantly put the diary back under the bed and walked slowly to the door, the words that she had just read resonating in her head. The teeth. The crypt. The castle. The land beyond the forests – that was Transylvania. Ellen didn't want any supper – she just wanted to know what was going to happen next. You didn't need to be a genius to work it out. It was harder to tell about the cousin, she didn't fit the profile quite so well, but there could be no doubt about the Count, it had been clear from Diary Day 1: he was definitely a vampire!